Chaos

A Novella and Stories

Edmund White

CARROLL & GRAF PUBLISHERS
NEW YORK

CHAOS
A Novella and Stories

Carroll & Graf Publishers
An Imprint of Avalon Publishing Group, Inc.
245 West 17th Street, 11th Floor
New York, NY 10011

AVALON
publishing group incorporated

ISBN-13: 978-0-78672-005-7
ISBN-10: 0-7867-2005-0

9 8 7 6 5 4 3 2 1

Book design by Maria Fernandez

Printed in the United States of America
Distributed by Publishers Group West

To my Michael,
without whom my life really would be chaotic . . .

Contents

I should like to put everything into my novel. I don't want any cut of the scissors to limit its substance at one point rather than another. Nothing happens to me that I don't put into it—everything I see, everything I know.

—André Gide
The Counterfeiters

Chaos

THE MORE HE HAD MONEY PROBLEMS, the more he prowled after men and boys online. His real problem was financial—he had to come up with four thousand dollars a month more just to meet his basic expenses now that his two pending contracts had fallen through. His money worries made him sit up wide awake at three or four every morning and rush to the computer to see if there was any good news coming in from London or Paris, cities that ran five or six hours later and were already well advanced into the work day.

He was also worried about his best friend, Marie-Hélène, who lived in Paris. She'd been complaining of sciatica and was now walking with a cane. Jack had had sciatica once when he'd lain flat on the bed and a hefty man had sat on his dick and Jack had made little plunges up into all this wet, soft heaviness—for the next week he'd scarcely been able to walk, so painful was his lower back. But that sciatica had lasted just a week; Marie-Hélène's had been going on now for two months and it was getting worse.

There never was any news about his books from Europe, good or bad, and usually Jack stayed awake another hour or two sending messages to young guys who wanted their cocks sucked. Some of them were other old men who couldn't sleep. A few were men in their thirties or forties who wanted a quickie on the way to work and if they did drop by the tension to get to their office on time made them come too quickly. But most of the men who were still up were crystal meth addicts looking for more drugs and someone sober enough (or on enough Viagra) to function as they all tunneled further and deeper into the heart-pounding dawn, unmemorable and exciting.

In a way, he thought, having sex on crystal must be the opposite of writing fiction. Fiction was constructed haltingly out of memories, actual or at least convincingly real, hybridized out of scattered recollections. Crystal meth, he understood, was agonizingly good, a sustained full-body orgasm, whereas writing was intermittent pecking, it was anxious work, two words canceled for every three put down, and all designed to bring pleasure or at least meaning to someone else in some place unknown to the author, someone reading in another location and time, perhaps carelessly, maybe with incomprehension or horror. If sex was an immediate rush so intense it became the only here and now and crowded out past and present, fiction was always written in the past tense and was lobbed like a paper plane over a cliff toward an unknown destination.

Jack didn't do drugs—no "420" (marijuana), no "PNP" ("party and play," in which the "T" of "party" was sometimes capitalized to refer to "Tina," the nickname for crystal meth or methamphetamine). Jack didn't even drink. He hadn't had a drink since 1982, when he'd published a successful book, an almost bestseller, and he'd realized he'd never be able to do the promotion properly if he was drunk the whole time. He had to stay sober to remember all the names, do all the breakfast radio shows, haul ass across America, making nice, chatting patiently with the eccentric little ladies who came to bookstore signings for the hors d'oeuvres, even just the miniature pretzels or broken chocolate chip cookies. "Sparrows" was the name in the trade for these freeloading little ladies, and Jack could never forget this association when he looked at their tiny claws darting forth, their heads bobbing and beady eyes fixing him and their sudden flutterings around the trail mix. He liked them, even their strange questions as irony-free and abrupt as bird chirping ("Now I take it you are no friend to the current administration: true or false?" a lady would ask, mumbling a peanut, following a reading from Jack's biography of Caravaggio).

That was the real world out there, the dismal empty streets in a Michigan town leading up to a brightly lit "Tony's Tomes" in a mall, where Virginia Woolf coffee mugs and quill pen and purple ink kits for calligraphy competed with a few actual books and action figures, where Jack's own reading might be relegated for want of space to the kiddy korner on the upstairs balcony. There he'd read to his bony, half-crazed sparrows perched on brightly colored children's chairs, surrounded by giant stuffed animals and freckled, life-size dolls with braids.

What did they think, all these oversized toys, of his *Remembering Our Gay Past: Queering the Adhesiveness of Yesteryear*?

Sometimes in the audience of stuffed toys and frail sparrows he'd see one stick-thin young man covered with dark KS spots and holding a cane (this was in the late 1980s). That was the only audience member who'd actually read Jack's books and traveled here through the sleet with a purpose. Once or twice Jack got away from his minders and had coffee with the young AIDS patient, someone with the ruins of good looks and a recently acquired mocking, superior manner despite his basic decency.

New York was totally isolated from that world of matronly women bookstore owners in floor-length Levi skirts and half-glasses dangling on a bright red velveteen cord, of unbathed, sleep-deprived radio announcers who hadn't read his new gay novel and just riffed on the title: "*The Middle-Class Man*—tell me, sir, are *you* middle-class? I can see you're a man."

New York, by contrast, on some days seemed to be made up entirely of men between thirty and forty, guys who knew all the names, who were gaunt from drugs, their closets filled with nothing but black clothes, their voices rich with knowing intonations, as if the flat tones of the Midwest had become more and more corrugated and sly the farther east each man had traveled. The New Yorker's intonations, if charted, would rise and dip as violently as the cityscape.

New York was already impossibly expensive, two thousand dollars a month for a studio just big enough to hold a bed and a chair, and most of the people he knew spent two-thirds of their take-home on rent unless they shared a four-room apartment with three other actors somewhere in Astoria, and that still cost each of them nine hundred dollars. Even so, crowded to the edge of the abyss, most of the young gay New Yorkers he'd met insisted on eating out four nights out of seven—not in expensive restaurants but in coffee shops or Subway or in Thai quickies or on takeout from Curry in a Hurry. On the way home from the movies or a night out dancing or when staggering away from hung-over days ten or twelve hours long as a showroom manager or as a leather tooler fashioning harnesses for sadists—at all these nodal points of the day they squeezed another twenty dollars out of an ATM and sat down to pick at food with a wolf-pack of other thirty-something guys. Or they borrowed still more money and bought some coke or Tina and rented yet another movie or watched *Saturday Night Live* reruns and laughed their way through them, then went online and found a second or third or fourth guy in the "party" mood and needed three alarm clocks and a phone call to wake up in time for work, but often enough they skipped sleep (or work) altogether. Nobody had any money, not even for basic expenses, but everyone was wasting more and more money on drugs, using a cash advance on one card to pay the minimum off on a second. Jack studied these glamorous, self-destructive spendthrifts at the Venus Coffee Shop, as they sat there dressed in treasured old white baseball jerseys with long green sleeves or baggy, sleazy teal-blue shorts which, if pushed too high, revealed a bright red jock strap and hairy legs, or white half-socks and brick-red lace-up shoes, one leg sometimes folded under a scrawny haunch.

They barely nibbled at their food, hiding half a burger or burrito under a lettuce leaf, because they were high and hunger-free, laughing with high-octane fury at a pun they weren't even sure had been intended while their glance raked the corners of the dining room looking for hidden cameras. The daily use of crystal had hollowed out their eyes, weakened their teeth in their sockets till they wobbled if touched, lent their skin the color and slack texture of wet paper towels, brought out pimples on frightened faces—and worst of all, had convinced them that their enemies were filming one long movie of their lives, a feature in five-thousand installments that concentrated on their sex lives (for why else did the air conditioner suddenly shift into freon mode just when Bobby was about to be fisted?), a series devoted to exactly their hottest, most depraved moments (that shadowy older man with the wire-rimmed glasses at the orgy last night was surely the porn director, for just as Tommy was getting pissed on by three jocks standing over him in a circle—*that* was the very moment the director aimed the remote at the TV, surely to start the hidden cameras rolling).

Right?

Right!

This was a porn film that would end up as a snuff film; at least Paul—beautiful Paul with the green eyes, long thick neck, long thin torso—was unshakably sure that he was being typecast as a victim, as a murderee by sinister forces closing in on him like seine nets tightening around small thrashing fish.

Sometimes Jack half-believed these stories of concealed porn and snuff movies being endlessly filmed. He had dinner with a friend of a friend, a nice, sane guy from California who came to New York twice a year to design sets for fashion week in Bryant Park. He said over the sweet Vietnamese coffee, "I just had the worst experience. Three years ago when I was in New York I hooked up with this eighteen-year-old dude fresh off the farm but back then? That night? When I was walking home I said to myself, This guy is going to be eaten for breakfast because he's naïve and he's got that fatal ten-inch dick. This time, yesterday? I hooked up with him again. Now he has a really nice apartment, a one-bedroom in Chelsea, but no official job, and he asked if I wanted to see a movie he'd made. It was of these identical-twin sixteen-year-olds who were stumbling around high on something and then in the movie? My trick was tying them up and gagging them and they were powerless to resist and next thing you know my guy was nicking them with knives and drawing blood and taking turns with the cameraman barebacking them and the camera would come in for a closeup as these poor kids were, like, sobbing? And screaming through their gags? The guy, the one I met three years ago and just hooked up with again? He said to me, like real smug, 'Yeah, we gave them roofies, they wouldn't remember shit, when we finished with them we drove them naked out into the country and dumped them, they'll never be able to report us.' I just said, 'Sweet,' and got out of there but now I'm thinking I should turn him in. If I do I'll have to stick around New York another week or more and lose business back on the Coast, but if I don't—well, how fucked up would that be?"

The point was that all these hotties—crazed and strung-out—could barely get to their jobs and if they did they couldn't meet their basic expenses on their after-tax paychecks but they blew every available penny they could borrow on drugs and on odd-hour restaurant meals they couldn't eat. And they were all sure they were going to be murdered brutally in a movie sold to such rich, secretive amateurs no one had ever heard of them.

In the eighties Jack had dated men strung out on cocaine who had holes in their shoes and ink stains on their dress shirts, who were months behind in their rent and whose electricity had been turned off, but who still, *still*, borrowed from friends and even banks to buy more coke (one of them had even resorted to armed robbery late at night on East Fifteenth Street, though he was pulling down a hundred grand as an advertising copywriter for Poli-Grip; he got a year on Riker's Island). But demented as those years had been, the coked-out eighties looked like child's play beside the crystallized first decade of the new century.

Being surrounded by all these drugs, Jack never felt the least temptation to join in. He even tended to avoid the guys who were really strung out—they depressed him. They twitched and smelled bad or they talked rubbish for hours on end. Jack was such a polite, careful listener that he couldn't tune people out. He had to choose good talkers to listen to, just as he had to select good books to read since he didn't know how to skim and was virtually a lip-reader.

Not all of the partiers he studied were desperate cases, or not all of them *yet*. Some of them could still work. Some of them still made it to the gym, listening to music through earphones as they ran on the tread-mill, faster and faster. They still remembered to call their parents on Sunday evening when they woke up from a heavily tranquilized sleep and ate Ramen noodles. Some of them could still take their laundry in one week and pick it up the next, could still make themselves bathe and shave every day and sober up on Monday, Tuesday ("suicide Tuesday") and Wednesday so that they could start partying Thursday night. So many of their friends did it that they in no way thought they were exceptional. Jack remembered in the seventies once when he was still drinking heavily, he showed up at a friend's house for dinner with a sack containing three bottles of wine.

"But it's just the two us," the host had said, troubled.

"Well," Jack had replied, blushing, "you never know who might drop in."

JACK was writing a novel about the life of Nijinsky. When Jack had been thirteen or fourteen his nutty mother had given him the life of Nijinsky to read written by Nijinky's wife Romola. Sometimes Jack thought while reading it that by introducing him to this book about the great queer ballet dancer, his mother had been giving him permission to be gay. Later when she reacted with rage and rancor to his confession, he realized he must have been misreading her.

Perhaps she hadn't really read the book herself—she could seldom alight long enough to read anything sustained. Surely if she'd picked it up she would have seen how explicit it was even for the period, especially about the impresario Diaghilev's passion for the much younger dancer with the thick legs and Tatar cheekbones.

"Diaghilev's boundless admiration for Nijinsky the dancer was even overshadowed by his passionate love for Vaslav himself. They were inseparable. The moments, in a similar mutual relationship, of dissatisfaction and *ennui* that came to others, never came to them, as they were so intensely interested in the same work. To make Sergei Pavlovich happy was no sacrifice to Vaslav. And Diaghilev crushed any idea of resistance, which might have come up in the young man's mind, by the familiar tales of the Greeks, of Michelangelo and Leonardo, whose creative lives depended on the same intimacy as their own."

To read that the two men "were one in private life" thrilled the fourteen-year-old Jack, just as he was half-convinced by Diaghilev's argument that heterosexuality was an animal necessity for breeding, "but that love between the same sex, even if the persons involved are quite ordinary, because of the very similarity of their natures and the absence of a presupposed difference, is creative and artistic."

Romola, Nijinsky's wife, bent over backward to be fair to her rival: "Yet Diaghilev was by no means entirely a sensualist. There was a strong esthetic pleasure in his affection for Vaslav, who always in his art and in his life was able to radiate beauty, to heighten emotion to the point of ecstasy . . ."

Because of the streak in his hair, Diaghilev was nicknamed "Chinchilla."

Yeah, Jack wondered now, but which one was the top? Probably Diaghilev was a pushy bottom, who got fucked but was very dictatorial about when, where and in what position. Or maybe Vaslav just kicked back and leafed through feelthy pictures of snowy-bottomed, black-stockinged ladies while the Maestro slurped away down between his legs.

For Nijinsky was straight, it seemed. Every time he slipped away from the Maestro it was to deck a little lady. Even Romola he never spoke to, since they had no language in common, but he used a (gay) intermediary (when they were all on a ship headed for the New World) to propose marriage to her: "Romola Carlovna, as Nijinsky cannot speak to you himself, he has requested me to ask you in marriage."

She hid and wept angrily, certain he was making fun of her, but when she understood that the proposal was serious, she joyfully accepted. She ran up to the deck and Nijinsky emerged out of nowhere and said in his primitive French, "Mademoiselle, voulez-vous, vous et moi?" Just as in a story ballet he pantomimed pointing to the ring finger and she cried, "Oui, oui, oui."

Jack realized that his character—and worse, his expectations—had been formed by such *l'eau de rose* reading. He, too, wanted to cruise a young man for days who'd appear on deck, brooding and indifferent—and then suddenly propose everlasting love. Jack, too, would call out, "Oui, oui, oui."

In the biography of Nijinsky by Peter Ostwald, Jack read that the dancer was just five feet four inches tall, that he could expand his chest sideways to give the illusion of soaring, and that his feet resembled those of a bird (though Ostwald, a doctor, questioned this detail). His leaps were so high that landing could be difficult. When he soared offstage in the last great single bound of *Le Spectre de la Rose*, it took four men to form a human net with their interlinking hands to catch him. His wife wrote: "As he stood there panting under the hissing klieg lights, his masseur massaged his heart and Diaghilev applied wet cold towels under his distended nostrils." His ability to *linger* in the air two or three seconds astonished his frightened and delighted audiences.

Jack relished all these details and struggled to fit them into a pattern. In the past he'd written directly from his own life or he'd invented stories from the beginning to the end. But in his Nijinsky he wanted to fit all the shards he'd collected into a smooth coherent surface, like *pique-assiette* ceramics made out of bits and pieces of broken, bright crockery.

One detail that fascinated him was Nijinsky's dance belt. After a triumph in Paris in 1910 with the Ballets Russes, Nijinsky returned to St. Petersburg to dance for the first time the role of Albrecht in *Giselle*. But instead of wearing the heavy pants associated with the role (Albrecht is, after all, a hunter), Nijinsky insisted on wearing what Igor Stravinsky described as "the tightest tights anyone had ever seen (in fact, an athletic support padded with handkerchiefs)." In Jack's youth gay boys who padded their crotches were said to be "ragging." In any event Nijinsky scandalized the Imperial Family who were in attendance. Reportedly a Grand Duchess herself asked that Nijinsky be fired for this impertinence, and yet many miles, many years and deaths later when in London and in exile the Duchess was questioned about the incident she claimed that she'd never said anything. "I was proud that such a great artist had brought glory to Russia and the throne and I would never have tried to drive him away." And it was all, it seemed, a mountain made out of a molehill, since Nijinsky's dick was disappointingly small. His first lover Prince Lvov had handed him on to Diaghilev because Nijinsky was a ball of sexual hangups (about masturbation and anal intercourse among other things) and, as the English dance critic Richard Buckle wrote, "He was 'small' in a part where size is usually admired."

He should have lived in the Internet era, Jack thought, when one could declare "Tiny Meat" in a profile headline and summon up thirty enthusiastic responses immediately from Chattanooga and Bangkok, Rotterdam and Dubai.

EVEN sober, Jack was as disorganized as the young men he lived among. He was sixty-six and his head was usually full of cotton wool and if he were left alone for a moment in a comfortable chair he'd sink into a deep, pleasant sleep, even if he awoke with a jerk three minutes later. People told him he smiled in his sleep—no wonder, since he often dozed off imagining a taut stomach so white it was blue against which a huge erect penis, so red it looked chafed, was throbbing as if it were a long muscular tongue attempting to lick clean a neat belly button, which was stitched to resemble a cross-section of a trilobite. Or he'd picture himself asleep on his side with Seth spooning behind him, his strong warm legs resting on him as if Jack's butt were two large ostrich eggs sure to hatch if only they received enough heat and pressure. No wonder his eyes crinkled in laugh lines. Maybe that was the function of old age—to convince the dying subject that sleep, eternal sleep, was more pleasurable than being awake. Old age was a deceptively cozy dry run for the chilling immensity of death.

In his waking life he was often so weary that he plotted out his movements to save steps. On a bad day he greeted every stimulus—the ringing phone, the arrival of the UPS man—with a groan, pretending even to himself he was writing and didn't want to be disturbed rather than admitting that his forces were flickering and even the most primitive form of motility (walking five paces to the bell) represented an expenditure of energy beyond his means.

On good days he said he'd never retire (nor could he in truth afford to), but when he returned to New York by train after two days of teaching he could barely haul himself to the top of the stairs in the station or on up to the street and the battle for a taxi. The escalators were always descending, mocking and boastfully free of passengers; everyone but the stationmaster knew that walking downstairs was never a problem, the challenge was to *ascend*. On Wednesday nights he sank into a hot tub with a pot of tea on the floor beside him and in his raised hands the newest *TLS* showing damp spots as he splashed about.

He made lists of things to do but forgot to consult them. Nothing yet was completely lost, but he had to write down his appointments right away or they would escape him an hour after he'd worked them out in detail and he'd have to make a humiliating second call ("Did we say Tuesday at three?" "No, a week from Thursday at four.").

Sometimes just the right tincture of coffee added to three drops of conversation, to the ozone-splitting of a bracing shower or the heart pump of a workout session or just the sudden, miraculous first day of cold in November—all these elements could fuse to pick the cotton out away from the boll, revealing the tough segmented carpels underneath. Then, free of all that sticky cellulose, his head would be as hard and articulated as when he was twenty.

But those days were rare. Ordinarily he'd feel as if someone had been feeding him slowly and secretly on an arsenic drip—or something more sinister and nuclear, which uncoupled neurons, backed up his digestion, thickened his ankles by pressing shut here and there a lymphatic valve or an arterial relay. If he went to a cocktail party (someone's book party, say), there he would be confronted with grinning, balding former students, a dozen other writers whose works he'd crowned with prizes or blurbed or ignored or reviewed badly or benignly, agents he'd once had lunch with twenty years ago and nearly signed on with—and he couldn't remember a single name. He knew all the details of their lives; the mere sight of their uplifted, lined faces and strangely colored hair instantly flooded his mind with details. He had an easy access to the stories about their aristocratic (if Jewish) family connections in Venice, to the subject of their thesis on bodily dismemberment in Renaissance sonnets, their recent battle with cancer, their affair a decade ago with a plump Mexican from Guadalajara, to a mental picture of their heavy furniture designed by a Viennese secessionist architect for a grandfather's dentistry waiting room. But their names?

He tried to work through the alphabet, hoping that as he played the gray, soundless keyboard one letter, a *k* or even an *n*, would slowly blush gold and ring forth its wonderfully precise vocables, as individual as the shape of the tooth to the tongue.

If he had to make an introduction he'd say the one name he might have excavated, "Beth Powers, I want you to meet a dear friend, who may look like a lady of leisure but is actually a great photographer who goes plunging out into the Sahara all by herself—no, she's fearless!—to take the most sumptuous photos imaginable. She's published a miraculous collection called *My Morocco*." At that point he'd go on smile remote and withdraw a fraction and Beth, afraid she'd missed the crucial syllables, would extend a hand and say, "I'm sorry, I didn't catch—"

"Helen. I'm Helen Hughes."

Jack's only hope was that after he'd recited so much detailed praise, Helen would find it unimaginable he couldn't recall something so basic as her name.

Sometimes, if not even one name floated up to the surface then he'd do the Parisian trick of saying, "I won't introduce you since of course you already know each other and I'm tired of presenting Proctor to Gamble or Goldman to Sachs."

Friends who were both tolerant and alert would pick up on his distress and introduce themselves while he feigned astonishment they'd not already known each other for "donkey's years" (one of the English affectations he'd retained despite a sickening wave of self-contempt every time he pronounced the words).

Names were gone. Worse, many memories, when invoked by others, had vanished—even quite delightful memories, apparently ("Remember that hilarious dinner we had with Michael Ondaatje in the Korean restaurant?" He'd say, "Are you sure it was Korean?" though in fact he couldn't place the dinner or cast of characters in any epoch, city, or restaurant).

In some of his books he'd written about early memories with such vividness that he'd become known for the intensity of these recollections, whether he'd fictionalized them or presented them as straight autobiography, but once he'd "done" these events on the page they had been drained of all their colors in his mind. He almost never reread his own books, but if a talk about his career required him to do so he usually felt nothing but embarrassment and awe before the fanciful if lucid intelligence he'd once displayed and that he knew he'd never be able to reproduce now. He'd become the stupid heir to his own younger, smarter self.

Sometimes the people he'd written about showed up years later, hugging him at receptions and laughing about the loss of their youthful beauty. "And you might like to know how that story turned out," Jim might say out of the Halloween mask of a face he'd carved and put on with the unruly bramble of eyebrows, the snow-white mustache, the unbelievably heavy black bags under the eyes and wrinkles so deep they looked like saber scars. "You know how you wrote about Annie and her family in Fort Wayne? Well, you'd never guess—"

And they'd tell him the suite to this forty-year-old anecdote, but a week later he couldn't remember the new installment. He'd forgotten it completely. All he was left with was the original question; the shiny surface of his brain had repelled the lately supplied answer, so long delayed and now thrown into the dustbin of oblivion. When people worked into conversation a phrase from his own writing, he never caught the allusion. Or sometimes it might sound familiar, but only vaguely, like one's own first name as pronounced by a Korean.

He'd receive e-mails from people he'd obviously been corresponding with for some time about their short stories or the conference on Russian ballet they were organizing or the urgent need to have their foreskins mistreated in a highly unusual way—and he couldn't remember who they were or what he'd agreed to do unless he looked up all his past e-mails to and from them. When the IT man where he taught accidentally erased fifteen thousand messages from his computer while pronouncing the fatal word, "Oops," he might as well have provoked a massive cerebral hemorrhage in Jack's brain: the memory banks had been wiped clean.

Jack almost welcomed the tabula scraped down and made rasa once more, though practically it meant he no longer knew when or even if he was going to be interviewed by the *Sacramento Bee* or whether he'd agreed to talk about sex and the memoir sometime next spring in Birmingham. As he'd lost his grip on his memory—the actual memory between his ears—he'd relied more and more on the virtual memory stored in his laptop between titanium covers. Now he was floating free of all those pointless interviews and colloquia, which no one ever seemed to remember anyhow a year afterwards, not even the people who'd presided or participated. When he'd first started out as a writer he'd imagined that he must control his own utterances in the self-important way Nabokov had practiced—he'd have to give typed answers to the journalists' questions, considered responses left every morning at the front desk of the Montreux Palace Hotel.

But as he'd lived through decade after decade of his desultory career and the dumbing-down of the nation, his name more celebrated than his books, his blurbs more solicited than his stories, Jack realized that by age sixty he'd given nearly a thousand interviews printed in magazines and papers in a dozen countries and languages and still only one out of every ten thousand serious readers had ever heard of him (and that one was sure to be an aging homosexual).

If he was so depressingly nihilistic about his persistent obscurity, it was because he lived in New York, the city that made reputations but couldn't remember them or sustain them. Like a great beauty who feels nothing though she inspires the men around her with life-changing longings, New York created desire but was frigid. If Jack had been the writer-in-residence at Cabo Lobos College or a state school in Normal, Illinois he'd have heard the pleasant *retentissement* of his fame all day every day; he'd have been venerated as a local big shot as he parked his Buick on Main Street and then perused the books at Borders, gravely visiting them like a priest paying house calls to pious invalids. In New York he was just one more semi-legend, another wannabe myth, a full-fledged heavenly sphere like Pluto in danger of being demoted to the newly created status of "dwarf planet."

He'd been diagnosed as HIV-positive in 1985 and feared that now he was—finally!—suffering (as a frighteningly high percentage of people with HIV did) from some sort of dementia, though maybe his wits were clouding over in the same way as his vision was dimming and his hearing was becoming less acute—it was all a normal loss of powers. Since he'd been diagnosed in his forties he'd never been able to separate the effects of aging from those of the virus.

Every loss was so subtle, such a seesaw up and down, that he couldn't track any definite decline. Not to mention that his conscious observing mind, the instrument he needed as the tracking device, was itself infected by the very diminishment it was meant to be studying. A philosopher had once said that to observe the mind at work was like attempting to sail a boat while building it; how much harder it was to sail when someone or something was angrily prying up the floorboards of the sinking hull.

Aristotle, who didn't have a word for consciousness, nevertheless could talk about the sensation of having (or not having) sensations. When we stare out into total darkness, he wrote, we can *sense* that we see nothing— a different feeling from being totally blind or closing one's eyes altogether. Jack wanted to know how his mind felt when it was minding nothing, not even the store. As he walked down the street or sat in the commuter train on his way to his university, he tried to stalk himself in the act of just being (this "just being" in his case recalled those long two minutes after a broadcast when the engineer would ask everyone on the set to be silent so that he could "record the room," for every silence has its own edge, depth, respiration).

The usual weather of his brain was small, dense, close. It kept swirling slowly around two axes—money anxieties and sex ambitions. Those weren't noble thoughts, not the high-minded questing he'd prized when he was young and would have preferred now. When young, his body produced so much energy that his mind was flooded with rapture or anger—feelings always too large for the occasion. Now his feelings were inadequate to the moment, feeble and *triste* when faced with the tragic, knowing and wry before the truly comic. It seemed that experience, neither late nor soon, ever provided the objective correlatives appropriate to the emotions.

He was better in conversation, for there he was so responsive to other people's quips and sallies, longings and conflicts that he became a joker or therapist on demand. He was "famous" in his little world as a conversationalist; it was wrong to call him a "chameleon" since those little lizards expended almost no energy apparently on changing colors, whereas Jack's adaptations left him both exhausted and exhilarated at the wrong end of the evening, a perfect recipe for insomnia. One of his friends said she preferred conversation to thinking because whereas her thoughts were beset by mental pictures, streaming videos of disturbing images, her conversation was just . . . words and more words, bland and sightless and automatic. Certainly words proliferating on his tongue were preferable to the tormenting images of panicked poverty he faced every night—or the nearly Pavlovian delights of his usual sex fantasies.

His sex ambitions were still the same—to have sex with every man in the world. He would have been a perfect whore since he found almost every man *do*-able. That was something Jack had learned from his first lover Charlie back in Chicago in the nineteen-fifties when gay life had been small and centered around the intersection of Clark and Diversey. Charlie never went home alone—that was a principle of his, a rule. He could always talk himself into finding something appealing about the last possibility of the day. "I like those thick black glasses—so nerdy, like Steve Allen's. Nerds are the best sex; they're so grateful. They're so awkward, so unpracticed, so overwhelmed that you might as well jerk them off as soon as you get them in the door—it just takes two or three strokes. Then while you're waiting for the recovery time to elapse and a new proper fuck, let them talk about their hobbies. Nerds have hobbies. They're the only people who have hobbies. Let them get it all out about their rare uncanceled five-schilling Austrian stamp. Let them show you their toy train. When they're bending over to fix the overpass bridge you can grab that big soft ass, even get some stinky-finger"—which he pronounced "stanky-fanger"—on the fairly convincing theory that all sex addicts were Southern.

"Sure, Charlie," Jack would say, longing to get him home alone. "But even you couldn't crack *that* nut," Jack would say, nodding to the four-hundred-pound bouncer with the porkpie hat and the short wide tie and the black stub of a cigar in his mouth.

"That man?" Charlie would exclaim, touching his own chest operatically. "Why, my dear, he's a highly attractive individual. He's heterosexual, to begin with, the father of three small children. He's in the Mafia and a killer, which pretty much meets my main benchmarks for masculinity. His cigar breath, his clammy rolls of hairy flab, his shit-and-piss-stained underwear, his utter contempt for the fag rooting around in his underbelly trying to locate his button-sized penis—why, he's the most thrilling *real* man I've seen all evening and how kind of you to draw my attention to his considerable charms." Charlie, often as not, would get the bouncer to stop his Lincoln in a dark alleyway and discharge in Charlie's mouth, or so he'd claim on the phone the next morning (Charlie was an advertising copywriter, which meant he could talk himself into buying any product, no matter how defective).

In a similar way awe and gratitude were Jack's main feelings during sex. As a five-year-old he'd sat on the lap of an air force pilot, Will Tommie, who'd unscrewed a pair of gold wings from his uniform and fastened them to the shoulder strap of little Jackie's pale yellow sunsuit. Jackie, whose own father never touched him and seldom spoke to him, nearly fainted from the contact with this young man's muscular body. Often afterward he'd felt like a child around a man, any man; he enjoyed sitting on the floor and giving a massage to some size-twelve foot or lying on his back while a young colossus stood naked over him, jerking off. He could sympathize with Jean Genet who in one of his poems imagined himself becoming no bigger than a thimble and traveling over the mountainous contours of his lover's body, even through his entrails, a tiny prospector holding aloft a lantern to inspect the monstrous, quaking, booming heart.

WHEN he first met Seth he'd complained to friends that their sex life was monotonous but by now, a year and a half later, that monotony seemed ecstatically *marital*. That was what he liked, that it was always the same, a predictable theme that could be richly developed through small variations. And their familiarity meant they were both so relaxed that they could forget about performance, about successfully arriving at the explosive conclusion, and could instead settle into a rhythm and wholly inhabit the sighing, sensual moment. Did Nijinsky submit to Diaghilev's eager mouth as Seth to Jack's? Seth was an ex-Mormon, just as Nijinsky had fallen away from Orthodoxy. But then Nijinsky had gone mad, believed he was Christ, carried a cross through the streets of Geneva. Would Seth revert, too, and float over Manhattan impersonating the angel Moroni? There were other differences: Seth had a big dick.

Seth was a tall twenty-eight-year-old whom the French would have called blond though his fellow Americans thought his hair was just light brown. As a little kid he'd obviously been a towhead. On a sunless winter day he could look as pale as week-old fish, but in the summer he became solar and in a strong cross light all the little hairs dusting his cheekbones glowed gold like tiny spears defending the craggy heights.

Seth was so masculine in a slouching, unselfcon-scious way that some of Jack's friends found him scary, as if Jack had done something weird like invite a white boy home to Harlem. In fact Seth in his acting days had always been cast as a straight man, even in gay plays. To be sure many gay men his age had perfected a "straight-seeming" manner, the one specified in the personal ads, but their very woodenness showed them to be fakes, just as their skinny legs—and their torsos *armored* in non-functioning muscle—revealed they were weightlifters, not jocks.

Seth had strong legs. Jack was convinced that he carried half his body weight in his legs. He had small eyes with nearly invisible lashes, a long nose with neat buttonhole nostrils, a big mouth and perfect teeth, but all inscribed in the lower half of his face. His neck was as wide as his head and nearly as long; when he turned his head to one side, complicated muscles came into play and rippled above his nape. His torso wasn't long or highly developed and his shirts were small or medium though he was six foot three and not skinny in any way. He himself said that he was tall only because his neck was so long.

He'd grown up a Mormon in Utah and Jack had fallen for him right after coming back from a month spent in the mountains two hours south of Salt Lake. Jack had been at a writers' colony where the wait staff had been mostly big Mormon boys in their early twenties, their tans set off by their mint-green Izod shirts, their slenderness dramatized by their baggy khakis. They trudged around like moonwalkers with their battered tin trays held high, which when empty they twirled on their fingertips like outer orbits. They were lean and blond and several of them had big, slightly bucked teeth, which made them look as if they were smiling all the time, even when they weren't. In truth they seldom smiled and they had million-mile stares; Jack couldn't tell whether they were stoned (highly unlikely, he thought, given their religion) or arrogantly standoffish or simply incurious about all the older Californians and New Yorkers they were serving.

They also seemed charm-proof; no matter how hard Jack worked he was never able to get any talk out of them beyond a half-polite murmur and nod. Maybe they considered non-Mormons to be boringly unsaved, of no interest unless they could be proselytized. Their indifference struck him as alluring. He'd observed a whole tribe of young people like them only once before—in Venice. The young Venetians (blond, confident, speaking the mushy consonants and hollow vowels in their baby-talk dialect) seemed supremely impervious to the hordes of foreigners milling around them, all those Canadians or Japanese following their leader's umbrella across the echoing piazza. The Venetians were the cabana boys at the Cipriani pool or the superb waiters at the Gritti or the jewelers on the Rialto Bridge—and they never remembered or even momentarily focused on a tourist. They lived in their own exclusive, isolated world—just like these Mormons, these Stepford husbands.

Jack and the other writers, during the month-long retreat in Utah, were fed in a big communal tent but housed in ski cabins scattered across the mountainside. The houses belonged to Mormon benefactors of the arts who were happy to surrender these chalets to writers, especially in the summer when they themselves traveled elsewhere. The houses were austere, underfurnished— and not one had a teapot or coffee urn, since caffeine was verboten. In several houses there were tintypes of unsmiling great-grandfathers wearing white beards with fanatical eyes so blue they looked empty.

The owners of the houses didn't want to know too much about the nature of the writing they were enabling; they'd learned that nearly everything in the secular world would strike them as offensive and impious. They preferred to imagine they were backing something vaguely uplifting. When the writers and the benefactors were brought together for one celebratory dinner it was a stiff, embarrassing occasion.

Soon after Jack came back from Utah to New York he was on Craig's List and looking under "Men for Men." There was nothing in the profile that suggested Mormon or gerontophile or that the young man was for rent, so it was only pure good luck that when Jack wrote the "twenty-seven-year-old six foot three top" that he wanted to pay him to suck his dick, it was Seth on the other end of the line. Seth wrote back, "Groovy, how about $120?"

That sounded low. Most of the boys asked for twice that amount and for a moment Jack wondered if the goods were somehow damaged. There was no photo— did he have AIDS and was his face wasted, his back hunched, his stomach bloated, his legs rail-thin, his arteries traced in high relief along his limbs? Or was he (Jack was always an optimist) someone who liked sex so much, whose dick was always so in need of a hot mouth, that he wasn't too picky? Maybe he preferred quantity to quality and wished to make it easy for the men who wanted him.

When he arrived, exactly on time, Seth was in good shape, though his face was a bit gaunt, his biceps no bigger than his forearms. But his body temperature was pleasantly warm, his feet hairless and beautifully arched, his ass smooth and full, his nipples protruding with excitement. He played the top, the total top with Jack, which pleased Jack since that way they could skip the whole discussion of whether one or both of them were positive; Jack was convinced that no one ever got AIDS from having his cock sucked. Later Seth would cheerfully admit that he was versatile and liked to "flip-fuck" with the right guy, only if the chemistry was right. Oh—and he was negative. Much later they had a three-way with a youngster with a big dick that Seth sucked while inches away Jack rimmed the kid's ass. Jack and Seth were so close they might have kissed. While Jack beavered away he watched Seth's mouth pistoning up and down. Seth's eyes were closed. "That was the most intimate thing we ever did," Seth whispered in the dark after the boy went home. Did Diaghilev and Nijinsky ever have a three-way? Jack wondered. Diaghilev would have held the small, dark, uncircumsized penis fastidiously between freshly ungloved finger and thumb while an eager new member of the corps de ballet rimmed the "god of the dance."

Seth didn't say much that first time. He seemed to lack color both in his personality and his skin tone. He didn't hang around long after he came. He splashed and dried himself off at the sink (he was so tall he loomed over it); he was friendly but not as easygoing as his straight-boy ways might have promised.

Jack asked, "Where do you live?"

Seth said, his eyes darting uneasily around the room, "Here and there. Mainly camping out with friends. But you can always message me."

"I don't know how to do that."

"Okay. Cool. Well, here's my cell—just leave a message."

Jack called him back a week later and wondered why he didn't find him more compelling. Seth was his type, or one of his types—tall, blond enough, masculine, dominant. Not that he dominated Jack at any moment except during the actual act of sex. Jack liked to make a spit-slick tube with his hand and extend this wet tightness with his open mouth; it wore him out and hurt his jaw muscles to deep-throat a large penis for long stretches. But at certain moments Seth would take Jack's hand away and make him open wide and go all the way down. The specific command wasn't what excited Jack; it was the insistence, the risk taken that he might make Jack gag and he didn't care: the strong preference.

Jack had no preferences. He liked coffee as much as tea and drank either with milk, or milk and sugar, or neither. He liked the right side of the bed as much as the left, a cool room at night as well as a warm one. As a boy he'd trained himself to sleep without a pillow because he'd read Napoleon went without one in his military tent; now Jack slept on seven, so high that he ended up half sitting up in bed.

He'd lived in Paris a third of his life but he didn't miss it, any more than he'd missed New York in Paris or Rome after he'd spent a year there. Was he a Buddhist, indifferent to the world and its allure? That didn't seem likely, anxious about money and attached to sex as he was. Then did his flexibility mean he was a world citizen, merely amused by local variations on universal themes? Too flattering an interpretation to be true. An Israeli woman friend of his, however, said he was a survivor like her who knew how to adapt. She'd grown up speaking Hungarian and Romanian then, after age ten, Hebrew, then English then French and German; he spoke "only" three languages but in growing up gay in the nineteen-fifties in America he'd had to pretend to be straight. "That's where it comes from," she said triumphantly, "your wonderful adaptable nature. I tell people who speak only one language or who won't leave their village, I tell them, 'Then just die! Leave some space for the living—you're already dead!' You're like me, completely alive and adaptable."

He wasn't sure he wanted to be such a ruthless, hearty survivor.

Nor was he passive like Chekhov's character "The Darling," who molded herself to each of her successive husbands' opinions, tastes and habits so adroitly that she could scarcely remember all the things she'd espoused in her previous incarnations. Tolstoy had thought "The Darling" was the perfect embodiment of Woman at her best, though Chekhov had intended the story to be satirical.

During sex and the moments that surrounded it Jack could be worshipful, even servile. Servility turned him on. He spent half a day doing three loads of Seth's laundry and folding his amazing collection of vintage T-shirts, rolling his white athletic socks and pressing smooth his boxer shorts and jockeys. Just as he was eager to sleep on the uncomfortable couch in order to surrender the king-size bed to Seth, a ridiculously light sleeper—but only because he knew that at three A.M. or five he'd wake up feeling the head of Seth's dick on his lips since Seth was as horny as he was sleepless.

This "service" Jack offered (and his naturally sweet disposition) didn't mean that alone he'd listen to Seth's favorite band Nine Inch Nails or hang out with Seth and his friends until late in the early morning hours. But it did mean he'd buy every one of Seth's preferred CDs and play them while cooking dinner for him in his presence.

His idea of sex had very little to do with his own penis, as small as Nijinsky's, and sometimes Seth, sensing that, ordered him not to touch his own erection, thereby turning a potential cause for embarrassment into a sexy compliance to a command—officially "sadistic" but actually compassionate. Seth's dick belonged to both of them and Seth's climax was something they shared. Sometimes Jack said to himself that only Seth could keep up with him and only he had as strong a sex drive as he did, but that was true only by courtesy. If Seth came five times a day, Jack could swallow semen just as often, but sometimes Jack barely got hard, much less had an ejaculation. The baby cries for milk five times a day and the mother lactates on demand, but that doesn't make the baby into a mother.

Seth had no interest in women sexually, which was unexpected in someone so masculine. Well, not really. That was more of an attitude of Jack's from the nineteen-fifties. Seth had a few women friends, most of them from the theater, and a handful from the Program, other recovering drinkers or addicts. Jack never met any of them, nor did he obtain a clear picture of them. At first Jack had thought it was he who was avoiding meeting Seth's friends. Then he realized that it was Seth who never wanted to meet Jack in a public place or go with him to a restaurant. Jack refused to be offended since it suited him.

Seth was, in a sense, too messy, too *doggy*, to be a ladies' man. He forgot to shower sometimes several days in a row, he lived in the same sweats and forgot to shave. Since this undeodorized neglect was one definition of "hot" in their gay world, "the natural, sweaty smell of a real man" in the personals, Jack was never sure whether it represented conscious coquetry or depression.

Certainly he seemed proud that he wore the same smelly shoes every day and when Jack would untie them and pull them off, Seth would press his dirty white socks against Jack's face—he knew Jack liked that (or knew it as much as anyone knows the always shifting sexual kinks of another person, today's thrill tomorrow's disgust). Jack had been drifting toward masochism for years, but Seth stopped the freefall. Seth wouldn't hit him, or at least wouldn't slap him or lash him with the belt Jack put in his hand with a coaxing little smile.

"Dude, I've got to come up with that on my own," he'd say, as if he were rejecting a piece of trashy "business" an autocratic director was trying to impose on him. Once when Jack succeeded in provoking Seth into an outburst of violence, Seth felt bad. He said, "I don't like that shit." Where some young guys seemed to find being the master empowering, Seth disliked it. Not that the play-acting demands were too daunting; he enjoyed darting into and out of fantasies. Administering a punishment broke his code—he had a very strong code that he never talked about but that revealed itself in action: he had his limits and Jack tried not to test them.

Actually Seth was very nice to him. He was even proud of him, though he'd never read anything Jack had written and made a point of remaining entirely ignorant of his work, just as Jack never read Seth's lengthy discussions of music on MySpace. In his own way, however, Seth was proud of Jack; at least Jack had once overheard Seth saying to another boy, "You know who he is? You don't? Don't you know he's famous? Well, sort of famous."

For the longest time their . . . friendship? . . . whatever it was, it didn't really take off. Jack liked him, Seth was able to drop in late and he didn't want to stay long, and those rhythms suited Jack, who had dinner with old friends every night or attended the opera. Gradually they became important to each other. Once a young writer had said to Jack, "I don't want to sleep with you— I want you to take me seriously." Which only made Jack smile; even the most brilliant new writer could hardly be expected to penetrate the fog in Jack's brain. When a talented protégé e-mailed Jack a story that he hoped Jack would pass along to the editor of a little magazine (which Jack had already done successfully once for an earlier story), Jack had to write him back and ask him to supply his last name—the erased computer made it impossible to recover it. This, after knowing the young (straight) writer for four years. Jack had even cooked dinner for him and spent a weekend with him and his girlfriend.

Despite a lack of ardor, he and Seth became attached to each other. Six months after they met, Seth's father died in his early fifties from a heart attack, induced by years of abusing cocaine. Or was it a suicide? Jack was astonished by how quietly Seth submitted to this unhappy fate, as if Seth had always inhabited a world of high Racinian tragedy instead of the low Feydeau farce Jack felt he himself was starring in, dashing under beds and into closets . . .

Seth didn't weep in Jack's arms or look to Jack as a father substitute. Nor did Jack ask how a Mormon in good standing could abuse drugs—he knew how lowering obvious questions could be.

Alone, Jack watched a documentary about crystal meth, about how widespread its use had become west of the Mississippi, about how it flooded the pleasure centers of the brain with ten times more dopamine than any natural event could ever release, about how it modified the entire brain chemistry, about how only a tiny percentage of users ever escaped its hold.

He was proud of Seth for his six months of sobriety, then his year, and at each juncture Seth received a poker chip from CMA (Crystal Meth Anonymous), which he flashed toward Jack, palming it for a second in his direction. No big deal—except it was a very big deal. Jack's eyes were so cloudy with cataracts he might have missed it, but he didn't.

Everything about their connection was curious, almost inexplicable. They would get together to "have sex" because Jack or Seth would announce he was "horny." But Jack usually kept on his t-shirt and shorts. He knelt on the carpeted floor between Seth's legs that were bent over the edge of the bed while Seth watched porn of a very "hard" variety in which skinny, assless men who seemed to be "tweaking" fisted or fucked each other. Or they pissed gallons and gallons of water on each other, sometimes through the bars of a cage, sometimes in a chorus standing around someone reclining naked in a tub and moaning. An off-camera man bellowed monotonously, "Yeah, baby, show him what you want. Swallow that load, piggy," all said in a rough, insinuating parody of the singsong used to encourage children or reassure frightened animals. Tough, save for the occasional leaking sibilance or the sudden upshift into a squeal or the matronly swoop of a diphthong . . .

If Seth would take a long time coming, Jack would whisper, "I could do this all night. Don't come too soon," but he himself didn't know if he meant it or was just being reassuring. If Seth said, "I already jacked off three times today and fucked a guy I met online," by way of an apology for his "Hollywood loaf," his half-hard erection (did that expression come from the exhausted LA cocaine culture?), then Jack would say something polite like, "I can smell his ass on your dick," or "Your cock still tastes of dried come," as a way of turning what might be regarded as a failing into an advantage.

And honestly Jack didn't know what he was doing or why. Was he paying out a hundred twenty dollars three times a week just to exercise his skills at reassuring others? Did he crave this contact with another human body as monkeys need their real or terry cloth mothers (then why not hire a masseur at the same price for a more thorough working-over)? Did he return to Seth again and again because he needed to tell himself and others that he had a "boyfriend," especially one young and desirable? All his life he'd pursued lovers or had them pursue him, and this was an activity familiar to the point of necessity, a focus for his days, even something like a luxury if *le luxe* is defined as useless but highly conspicuous and necessary consumption. He was still alive. He hadn't died yet.

He suspected that within him there was some other half-secret plot afoot. If Jack was honest with himself he had to admit that he wanted Seth to fall in love with him. He knew perfectly well that he wasn't Seth's type—forty years too old, fifty pounds too fat. And if one isn't a recognized character parading about on the stage of another man's imagination, there's no way one could ever become his love object. Friend, yes. Even best friend. An "adorable" friend (Seth had called him adorable more than once). Fuck buddy, possibly. John, certainly.

Seth always made him pay for it, even when Jack invited him on an all-expenses-paid holiday to Greece. Even when it was Seth who knocked on his Athens hotel room door at five in the morning and whispered, "I just fucked two guys in the park behind the parliament building and jacked off twice but I'm still horny."

Jack wasn't stingy. He knew that it was normal for a man in his sixties to pay a beautiful youngster in his twenties for what the online personals called "friendship with benefits." Now that Jack was so broke Seth had even lowered his rates from a hundred and twenty dollars to a hundred, which was nothing in a city where that was the going price for a dinner for two in a mediocre restaurant—and this was fine dining. If Jack wanted to trick Seth into having sex (just once) for free, it was because he wanted Seth to love him. In his journal Jack wrote, "Which tells me that I have a magical fantasy that a young man is going to love me all over again and want me 'forever.'"

Maybe that was the point—if love were forever then how could either partner ever die?

Nijinsky wasn't gay but he was proud to be "le petit," as Diaghilev called him. They were collaborators—and the Maestro even let the Little One use up endless rehearsal time choreographing "The Afternoon of a Faun" in which Nijinsky rubbed one off onstage using a veil that a nymph had dropped. He'd even entrusted Stravinsky's magisterial, revolutionary "Rite of Spring" to Nijinsky's herky-jerky spasmodic choreography, so incoherent that Nijinsky had to stand on a chair in the wings shouting out long chains of numbers to the dancers while the audience booed and threw things.

Did Diaghilev hope that somehow this troubled, small-dicked half-Polish hard-headed Little One would love him, truly, deeply? Would get drunk one night and rape Diaghilev's mouth, fucking him so hard his monocle would pop out and his celluloid collar jump off its button and spring open? Instead, the Little One dropped Diaghilev with apparent ease, married Romola and started his own ballet company—though soon enough the Little One descended into madness. He bought a big knife and locked himself in his hotel room. When a psychiatrist forced the door open, Nijinsky became creepy-crazy-campy.

The shrink reports: "In a grotesque way he enacts for us the unexpected surprise. 'I am a man of the world and not accustomed to being treated this way.' He makes use of a peculiarly scanning and saccadic speech style, articulating slowly, with exaggerated clarity, and accenting the individual syllables and words with irregular and unfitting pauses, all in a pompously serious and lofty tone of voice, accompanied by stiff mimicry." Jack read elsewhere, in Joan Acocella's brilliant introduction to the Nijinsky Diaries, that he exhibited another feature of schizophrenic speech—"clanging, the connecting of words on the basis of sound (often rhyme) rather than sense, and perseveration, or persistent repetition." Clanging, it seemed, was something like: "Give me some wine, I will be thine, try to take mine, why don't you shine, fine, line . . ."

The description had a chilling effect on Jack, since he could imagine going mad in just that way, a figurine on top of a music box, slowly turning and saluting and bowing—slower and slower as the box wound down while he'd go on offering nonsense riffs on accidental rhymes.

But Jack wasn't winding down. Full of HIV pills and vitamins and juiced up on androgen gels, he had an unremitting energy; if he drifted off to sleep in his armchair he was awake again a minute later, as if he were wearing the Red Shoes and must keep moving. But he knew his days were numbered and that the number wasn't a winning one. Soon he'd be seventy. A dinner and a doze later he'd be eighty. Which wasn't good. There was nothing good about eighty.

He'd known a few very gallant eighty-year-old *mondains* in Paris who still went out every night, impeccable, *à la page*, charming, even energetic. His friend Marie-Hélène had once chided him when he started yawning even before the cheese course arrived: "*Nous les mondains ne sommes jamais fatigués*" ("We socialites never get tired"). Though he teased her about it afterwards he agreed with her; that was still his credo—we're never tired.

He used to see the Baron Rédé in his perfectly tailored suits and his tiny varnished shoes tottering out at age ninety with his beloved, Juliette Greco's equally ancient sister, the two of them billing and cooing with perfect complicity in "their" booth at the Voltaire. When the Baron would have Jack to lunch he'd talk to him about the latest novels in English and French; he was up on his Jonathan Franzen and his Zadie Smith. Like all Parisians he worshipped the Latest Cry, the Newest Genius, and this religion at least had the virtue of keeping them all interested in the world around them. There was nothing sadder than someone out of synch with his entire epoch.

If the middle class in France had striven for two centuries to become aristocratic, the aristocracy had always been determined to stay young—fit, fashionable, up-to-date. In Paris you ignored the latest fad at your own risk and you revisited the *recent* past at your own peril (the *distant* past could always be recycled).

THEY went to Naxos together and used it as a base for other excursions.

Jack wrote in his journal: "Seth and I just got back from Mykonos. Unlike Naxos, it's an island full of gay sexual possibility and Seth went off exploring 'Paradise Beach' and the four or five gay bars (without any luck, which means no one would have much luck, if a twenty-eight-year-old six-foot-three Mormon blond strikes out).

"He and I get along great. He likes to have sex three times a day and he asks me if I can keep up with him and I can. He's smart, observant, creative. He appreciates people and places. I've always been alone with him for the past year. Suddenly I'm seeing him with English ladies, nine-year-old girls, American friends—as well as waiters and bartenders—and everyone likes him. He's charismatic due to his looks and his charm. He has that long, muscular neck, small dark eyes, a full mouth, straight nose, huge knobby Adam's apple, warm skin, blond body hair that becomes brown around his crotch, high-arched size-thirteen feet that don't look big given his size. He weighs two hundred and five pounds.

"He's very interested in half a dozen bands—Radiohead, Muse, Guillemots, Nine-Inch Nails. He's turned off by singer-gurus like Morrissey or Michael Stipe. If he likes a song he'll write an extra verse in that group's style. Strangely, he also likes show tunes, Streisand hits—he studied musical theater.

"He's polite, considerate, reliable, but on some deep level reserved because I'm not the one for him, not even a possible candidate, though he admits we have good sex. I wouldn't dream of sharing a bed with him all night.

"He knows I'm always eager but that I know my place.

"Mykonos is no longer the gay safe house it once was. It's now mostly taken over by tens of thousands of Italian teens all raising hell and racing past on motorbikes, or curling up against one another like puppies in the morning as they wait for the ferry, or clowning around and getting drunk. The road to Paradise Beach is littered with smashed motorbikes, and the hospital is full of Italians who've had accidents. Naxos feels peaceful by contrast."

"I GUESS I really am in love with Seth. What I said to him as a 'line' really has become true—that we're usually friends but that without a transition we can move over into passion, dirty sex, total pleasure.

"There are many constraints on this love (one-sided surely). He won't let me get away with having sex a single time (even if we do it three times a day) without paying him something.

"And then his type is young and skinny and arty (at least I'm artistic). He said to me, 'You know you're adorable, don't you?'

"'No.'

"'You're—what? Sixty-six? But you act like a little kid.'

"My main fantasy is to lie in the little niche next to Seth's room. If he becomes horny during the night he promises to wake me, lead me by a collar into his room and fuck my face. Last night just talking about it prompted him when we got home to steer me around with his belt around my neck and in that way guide my face down to his crotch.

"And then he's been so unhappy; both his parents abandoned him at one time or another, his brother abused him, he (Seth) became a crystal addict, and his father just died after a life of sniffing coke (and dealing it). All this suffering and deprivation and his still-new sobriety (fourteen months)—all make him wary, detached, paranoid. When he first met me a year ago he thought I was one of a group plotting to kill him.

"And yet, and yet. He's a funny guy who appreciates things and accepts people, who knows how to find and give pleasure. He loves to joke and in just eight or nine days of being constantly together we've put together a whole repertory of silly or nutty references. He was fascinated by our hostess, her grand upper-class accent, her dry, sometimes cutting humor, her sudden bursts of intimacy and warmth. He likes 'hanging out' with an American friend though he might have seen him as a rival or threat. He's a genius at sex, which begins with generosity and is fueled by great appetites. Today he came five times in the last twenty-four hours. Because he's generous he's helped me realize all my fantasies. But there are things he won't do—he doesn't like anything sadistic and he was wounded when I said during a fight (a very little fight), 'I suppose it's stupid for me as a masochist to complain I'm being mistreated.' He mulled that word over and said half an hour later, 'I've never wanted to mistreat anyone. I've been mistreated too much myself. Anyway, I've never mistreated you.'"

AFTER the trip things changed. They grew a lot closer. Seth confided in Jack, and more importantly joked with him. Jack saw expressions on his face he'd never glimpsed before, a new riskier way of baring his teeth in laughter, not just the tip but the whole tooth revealed. He'd talk in funny voices, now an old-fashioned impresario announcing his boy magician in formal terms, now a junky nodding off over half a joint burning his fingers and making his eyes tear.

They started playing young Mormon pioneer Jebediah and his bonneted, freckled wife Martha. It all began one night after sex. Seth had been slow to come. Jack had put guests in the big room so he and Seth were crowded onto a single bed in the little room without the TV or access to porn. Maybe Seth had trouble getting excited without porn—or maybe without it he was more intensely in the moment than ever before. How strange it was that this language of sex is so crucial to most people (we hang on every word the body pronounces) and yet we're not sure, not sure at all, what's being said.

They were both tired. Neither of them had slept more than a few hours in the last three nights. Jack, for once, was not at all detached or busy mentally commenting on the action. Fatigue had tricked him out of irony and detachment. He was just a mouth, and Seth was this big, rangy, warm, hairy body cast athwart the bed.

In Jack's mind they were a Mormon couple, both young, just married, living in a tall wood house isolated in the midst of hundreds of farmed acres. The man was Jebediah, fierce and taciturn with the callused hands of a worker, a big mouth that never smiled, and small, suspicious eyes, someone who read nothing except the Book of Mormon. He wore his long underwear, his "garments," which he'd been given when he was nineteen and admitted to the Temple, and his big, hard penis jutted out of the immaculate white flap. His wife knelt beside him and sucked him as he'd instructed her to do. There was no sound outside the house or inside except the creaking of the old cherrywood bed. She knew she had no choice but to obey; it didn't quite seem right to her that this big thing, still tasting of urine sometimes, should dig so deep down her throat with no regard to her comfort, or that it should discharge so copiously and flood her mouth with its hot stickiness.

By day Jeb paid her no mind and seemed scarcely aware of her existence. She'd put the food on the table, he'd recite the blessing—and nothing more was said until he scraped his chair back and dropped his napkin on the cloth. The rest of the time he was in the field or doing chores.

They went to bed early and he never, not once, forgot to feed her his penis, no matter how hard he'd worked planting or scything or winnowing. Nor did he ask her if she was in the mood. She was too afraid of him to protest in any way. Maybe it was his idea of birth control, but why would he not want a whole tribe of little Jebs to do the farm work?

They undressed separately and she put on her night-gown out of sight, flannel in the winter and cotton in the summer. He extinguished the light and a minute later he threw the sheet and blanket back and pulled the big hard thing out of his flap. If she didn't make a move he'd push her head down there.

He was so quiet and so superior to her that she came to prize the occasional groans of pleasure that would escape him, tight-lipped as he was, his eyes closed but sometimes wincing with bliss. She learned he liked it if she licked the shaft and tongued the head, if with one hand she lightly cupped his testicles. She hardly knew if it was a sin or a form of disobedience to introduce vari-ations such as these, but she prided herself on her ability to please such a great man, to make him vulnerable to, at least, his own sensations.

He was clean when he came to bed; they both washed themselves off with a wet cloth before donning their nightwear. She could sometimes smell the slightly mildewed odor of the washcloth on his skin and could feel the superficial coolness that his ardor would soon enough burn away.

At first she thought there was something monstrous about what he expected her to do, night after night. In her virginal dreams her future husband had romanced her and nibbled her ear and let his hands brush past her sensitive nipples. Then, in the dead of night, while she feigned sleep, he would lift her nightgown and enter her ever so gently. The rapture of such a penetration, occasional and always nocturnal, was God's way of begetting children to populate the New Zion.

Not this monstrous spilling of seed, this throat-rape, this sterile, tranquil, unremitting violence worthy of Onan.

And yet she liked it now. Her breasts would swell and her nipples become achingly sensitive—

AND on and on the fantasy would unscroll in Jack's mind, this solemn sexual saga of the Rockies. He made Seth blink when he started to tell him all that, and Seth just laughed and said, "Well, what an imagination. You should try writing fiction."

Once or twice Seth signed himself "Jeb" in an e-mail, but Jack knew that in some unexamined way he didn't want to commit a sacrilege against the Mormonism he no longer believed in but that his brothers espoused and his mother was returning to. After Seth's father's death the whole clan had begun to close ranks. Seth's mother, who'd run a dude ranch in Montana for years and even appeared as a cowgirl on the cover of a national magazine—his mother was selling her house and returning to Salt Lake. Seth's little brother was about to set forth on his two-year mission to Thailand (a destination a mite too full of temptations, Jack suspected, for a kid with a blond, frizzled Mohawk, a Mo-Fro).

Nor did Seth really like the man-woman thing as role-playing. Some gay men liked pussy-talk, make-you-my-bitch talk, half whorehouse, half prison, but Seth wanted to be just some guys together fooling around. That's what he got into, buddies hooking up and getting off. But sometimes on his way out, he'd say,

"Be obedient in all things, Martha," and he'd lower his eyes, embarrassed or was it amused or just tolerant (in an unfamiliar way) of his friend's folly?

JACK showed a hundred pages of his Nijinsky novel to his editor, a bloodless man in his forties who seemed to have just awakened or to have just molted his shell and was feeling so vulnerable he decided to hide until he grew back something tough. Jack had always liked him. He was frail and didn't talk about sports but he did joke a lot in a brainy University-of-Chicago way that Jack could never quite follow. The editor had an immoderate appreciation of James Joyce, especially *Finnegans Wake*.

He was thin and exhausted and always laughing tepidly, but for all this pained sensitivity he managed to crank up what appeared to be genuine enthusiasm only for books about food and wine. Jack had noticed that heterosexual men approaching the climacteric redirected all of their obsessiveness (especially if their wives had curbed their sexual drive) toward cooking and drinking. What might have appeared in an earlier generation to be gluttony and alcoholism now dressed itself up as epicureanism and oenophilia. Maybe because Jack had lived in France so long and knew all too well the very limited, finally trivial joys of gastronomy, maybe because he'd had to stop drinking but still ate too much and too richly, he was unimpressed by the *refinement* of expensive feeding and "beveraging" (as a Southern friend called it). Yes, booze and food were among the "arts of the table," but they weren't art, for Christ's sake, not real art.

These middle-aged straight editors, though, were shameless "foodies" who sent dishes back to the kitchen the way knowledgeable Frenchmen used to refuse wines that tasted of the cork. These editors still made their wives cook macaroni and cheese for the little girls six nights out of seven, though on the seventh day Daddy got out his green peppercorns and Grand Marnier and the preserved lemons and the hundred-dollar cut of beef and the special knives from Henckels and dirtied every pan, dish and lemon zester in the place.

Jack's editor was always in full cry after the latest chef and could talk at tiresome length about a wine's "raspberry tessitura" and its "mossy undertones," just as he could swoon over an Earl Grey sherbet on a wedge of pignoli pie served on a teakwood slab, or radicchio ravioli stuffed with shark's fin puree and brushed with elderberry foam. He used his dinners with writers as an excuse for running up big wine tabs and chatting with the chef, who invariably came out to pay his respects to an editor who might yet make him famous.

At the end of the dinner at the new fusion Cuban-Vietnamese restaurant in which the sticky rice was decorated in "its" black-bean coulis, the editor said casually to Jack, "I glanced through your pages on Nureyev."

"Nijinsky."

"Right, and frankly I don't think readers today can tell one from another. I'm afraid we're just going to have to drop this one and eat our losses."

He was nibbling a coconut flan decorated with tiny black anise fruits that had been somehow charred and caramelized.

"You didn't like what you read? " Jack asked. "You want me to revise the second chapter, the part where I talk about Prince Lvov? You want me to cut straight to the chase, the good stuff, the Petroushka opening night in Paris where Diaghilev—"

"No," the editor drawled, "it's all very well-written of course, but I ran it up the flagpole and no one saluted."

"Did you like that bit," Jack asked, excited, "where I said Diaghilev dyeing his hair black but keeping the white stripe in was just like Sontag—the stripe as metonymy?"

"You don't understood, Jack. It's over. Time to move on to something else. Case closed."

"You're not going to do the book?"

A feeling of dread came ringing down over Jack like an isolation booth around a contestant. He'd always felt so comfortable with his neurasthenic editor, whose only flaw seemed to be his constant need for a transfusion.

"What do you think of this petite Sirah? Quite sociable, wouldn't you say, as a vino da tavola?"

He'd forgotten Jack didn't drink.

Jack suddenly *dreaded* his editor, who until now he'd always thought of as a younger brother. Now he looked more like an enemy.

As Jack walked home through the light autumn rain (he suddenly felt too poor to hail a taxi), hot tears sprang to his eyes. Here he was, way up in his sixties, the author of twenty books, the subject of several dissertations, and his publisher was just dropping his novel, not because it was bad but because none of the dimwitted twenty-somethings in the mailroom had ever heard of Nijinsky.

He didn't call his own agent but he did speak to a knowledgeable woman friend who worked in the business. She said, "No more gay fiction. Gay people aren't loyal to their own authors. No more fiction, for that matter—you should *see* the sales figures that are coming in. Try a biography, but not a *literary* biography; no one cares about writers. The problem is finding a subject with lots of name recognition who hasn't been done to death."

"I've always wanted to write a big novel that would span three decades and map out the fates of a gay guy and his best friend, a straight guy—"

"Read my lips: No. More. Gays. No. More. Novels."

He said, "I have an idea for a novel—*not* a gay one. It would be about this Mormon couple in the nineteenth century living near the Great Salt Lake—"

"This wouldn't have anything to do with the Nijinsky idea, would it?"

"How do you mean?" Jack asked, confused.

"You wouldn't try to show Nijinsky touring Utah or something, would you? Anyway, Mormons sound like a bit of a stretch. Stick to a biography."

Who would he write a biography of? Clinton? Would Clinton authorize an elderly gay novelist of note to write his life? Feel flattered by his devotion? Whom did they know in common, Clinton and he? Who could arrange an introduction for Jack?

That would show them all. Millions of dollars as an advance. He'd be bankable again.

He said to his friend, "I could write a cookbook. I'm a famous cook—well, famous to my friends. I've been doing it for forty years."

"You've never had me over," she observed.

"I'll make you a Sardinian meal. There are no Sardinian cookbooks and I had a trick from Sardinia who taught me all these dishes, mashed sardines and pulse soaked overnight on a bed of dandelions—"

"Jack," she bleated, as if his name had become a complaint, "to write a successful cookbook, you need a TV show. A restaurant. An accent. A whole chain of restaurants. I like your Clinton idea better."

For the moment he had to worry about his dwindling bank account. He'd been wrong, in his salad days, to arrange for bills to be automatically deducted from his account. He'd never balanced a checkbook or even written down check stubs. He'd just glanced once a month at his bank statement and begun to worry when it dipped below twenty thousand. Now he was down to four thousand and every time he withdrew money from his ATM he checked his on-screen balance, something he hadn't done in years. A friend said he needed an "estate planner," which made Jack laugh since he had nothing to plan and was still expecting a miracle. To recommend a financial planner to Jack was like suggesting to a frog that he find a bigger pond when he was still hoping to be turned into a prince.

The editor had not only canceled his Nijinsky book but had dropped another proposal for a little guide to successful entertaining with chapters on feeding eight friends in an apartment of a hundred and forty-five square feet on a budget of fifty dollars and so on. Jack's oldest friend had done some sophisticated drawings in the manner of William Hamilton cartoons in the *New Yorker*, the men all tall with repp ties and glasses, the women carefully coiffed and dressed.

The bloodless oenophile editor had merely closed his eyes when Jack mentioned the entertainment proposal, as if waiting for noisy children to subside and play elsewhere.

"We could make it into a nifty little book," Jack said, a bit hysterical, "fun to handle, attractive to the eye and touch, and pile it up beside the cash register, ch-ching!" Jack was talking with fake bravado, though the editor's closed eyes made him lose heart and he almost whispered the final "ch-ching . . ."

He tried to interest Wesleyan, where his archives were deposited, in buying the manuscripts of his last four novels, but the librarian was using up a month's worth of "personal days" she'd neglected to spend in previous years. He contacted a speech agent he'd heard about in Ohio, but she said that Jack would interest no one but gay organizations and they'd all had him already for free, years ago. But did he know how she could get in touch with David Sedaris?

In late September he went to Paris to launch the French translation of an old novel. He was flown to Strasbourg and a waiting audience of two hundred people, then back to Paris the same evening. The next afternoon he was driven in a minibus to a waiting audience of a hundred in a recently restored abbey in Brittany. He appeared on an hour-long prime-time television book chat show that was broadcast live from a barge floating on the Seine; he was the only guest. It went well except the young, slender, self-amused emcee asked him on the air, "*Etes-vous un vieux cochon?*" ("Are you a dirty old man?"). Jack nodded with a bitter little laugh (a "yellow laugh" as the French said). He spoke for three hours in six half-hour sessions on France Culture, a national radio station devoted to the life of the mind. He received glowing reviews in twenty newspapers and six magazines. He engaged in an hour-long debate with Margaret Atwood before an audience of five hundred women in Vincennes. Everywhere he went he was told he was "brilliant" and that his book was a "masterpiece."

And when all was said and done his publisher sold fewer than three thousand copies. His editor, a dear old friend, shrugged and said, "They're pleased with the results," but Jack didn't see how they could be. He felt that he'd been introduced personally to each individual who'd bought his book.

While he was in Paris he saw his friend Marie-Hélène every day. On the way over from his hotel in St. Germain to her apartment on the Place Maubert he'd pick up a creamy quiche lorraine from Mulot. Marie-Hélène was on a cane but she'd washed the salad greens and set their places in the sitting room with its gold wallpaper and gleaming hardwood floors. Neither cat really liked Jack and he'd see just a sliver of gray fur or a big black face blinking bigger gold eyes. The cats would be darting under the couch or roosting on a distant Louis XVI chair in the study on a pale pink cashmere shawl.

When he'd first met Marie-Hélène in 1974 at a party in New York she'd been married to a painter best known for his sets for the opera, vast flats depicting baroque fountains and formal gardens in the moonlight or aerial perspectives of Versailles framed by ancient trees. He favored the dim palate of Poussin and the same startling patches of cobalt blue or magenta or chromium yellow, the sort of intense shades one sees only at sunset, though in Jean-Pierre's sets (or Poussin's paintings) it was always some later, dimmer hour.

Back then Marie-Hélène already was wearing around her shoulders her many exuberantly draped scarves from which protruded her ivory cigarette holder at a rakish angle. She always seemed to be encased in hobble skirts that underlined her slenderness and legginess. Her shoes were pagodas of miniscule gold buckles and red leather straps; she looked like Rapunzel teetering from the top of a shoe tower.

She often wore big round pale-blue sunglasses even at night or in midwinter. Her slightly burnt-oak smell of *Gauloises Jaunes* was contradicted by her early-spring honeysuckle perfume. She never varied her perfume— it was her trademark, as were the scarves and cigarettes and red shoes and her deep, broken voice. She was proud of her voice and worried that if she stopped smoking it would clear up and sound like everyone else's.

She had all the qualities that contribute to joie de vivre. Her stamina was unremitting. Her curiosity was boundless and three or four new books were messengered to her door every morning. She was always racing off to the latest play, opera, movie or art exhibition. She conceived of life as a series of battles, most of which she was winning. Her constant cry was, "Avanti!" Sometimes she changed it to, "Avanti, popolo."

She didn't really speak Italian but she did speak French, Spanish and English, but oddly enough she had an accent in all three. Her very low, raucous voice and her slow, careful enunciation made her French sound somehow foreign; French people often asked her if she was Swedish or German. In fact she was Jewish and French and during the 1940s she and her sister and her mother and aunt and grandmother had all lived safely in Mexico City while her father served De Gaulle in England. Her Spanish had the soft consonants and the little music, the cantileña, of Mexico, though she'd never much liked Mexico and had visited only once after her family had returned to Paris in 1952. While a teenager in Mexico she'd gone on wild dates with American soldiers stationed there, even black ones, and from them she'd learned a cool-cat version of English. Now, sixty years later, she'd spoken with so many hundreds of people in so many languages that she could scarcely finish a single sentence in any one ("*Quand même, mon vieux,* we're not licked yet, *avanti popolo,* there's always mañana").

She read Spanish mysteries in the morning, American epics in the afternoon, Hitler memoirs in the evening. She made the flattering assumption, which had become nearly an article of faith, that Jack read as widely and indiscriminately as she did. Like all religions, hers required more belief than truth, more wishing than observing, for Jack never read any genre fiction—no whodunits, no sci-fi, no romances—and he ransacked books of fact more than he read them properly. Fiction he read very, very slowly. He knew his way around books, counted many authors as friends and was a holdover from that era when writers had sent their books to one another and expected an eloquent, insightful letter of praise within the week. To this day the arrival of a book in the post filled him with anxiety since he saw it more as a social obligation than an artistic invitation.

Marie-Hélène had no such dread of the printed word. She went toward it as toward her own life, with gusto and delight. When he read Henry James's autobiography, *A Small Boy and Others*, he came upon a passage that reminded him of Marie-Hélène's confusion of life and art. Henry James and his brother William were never properly educated—they were always being pulled out of one school in New York and being whisked off to an *internat* in Geneva or a tutor in London or a school for foreigners wanting to learn French in Paris. Nothing was sustained or systematic, no more than had been Marie-Hélène's schooling in Paris, then, when her family fled before the Nazis, in Avignon, then in Mexico City. As a result, she was hopeless with numbers, had the most surreal sense of geography and couldn't spell in any of her languages.

But as in the case of James her very lack of normal instruction meant that she was unusually open to all the hints and lessons, the sheer pleasure, of books and painting. James writes that as teenagers he and his brother William (who hoped to be a painter) wandered by the hour through the art galleries of the Louvre, which was still an imperial palace at that point. Their glimpses of Géricault and David were a "foretaste of all the fun, confusedly speaking, that one was going to have, and the kind of life, always of the queer so-called inward sort." Their discoveries of "the great premises" were like "so many explorations of the house of life." Finally, he concludes, "The house of life and the palace of art become so mixed and interchangeable" that one could no longer be distinguished from the other, all these rich minglings occurring in the crowded Louvre, "the most peopled of all scenes not less than the most hushed of all temples."

It was a stretch, but Marie-Hélène seemed to him the same sort of mind whose personal experience was entirely aesthetic and her aesthetics invariably personal.

He was with her in Paris when she received a diagnosis of bone cancer that had metastasized throughout the pelvic area; in the X-ray her bones looked like lace. She said she felt as if an animal were gnawing away inside her hip—"Like a crab," she said, "because cancer is a crab." The pain, he knew from other people, was excruciating, but she spoke of it only as a technical problem requiring precise engineering. She had her morphine patches every day and other pills to fight the nausea and still others to counteract the constipation. She began her chemo almost instantly and a week later her hair was falling out; she devised magnificent turbans that were so theatrical that her face looked like a pale sliver of a moon spotted between the cloudbanks of her indigo shawls and the folded iridescence of her Tuareg-blue headdress.

Jack had lost so many friends to AIDS and death, even two lovers, that he thought nothing more could reach him, but Marie-Hélène's illness—her *terminal* illness?—frightened him as much as the prospect of his own death. They were so different—she so energetic and he so slothful, she so stylish and he such a shlub—that observers had a hard time understanding their friendship, starting with what they might have in common. Books, yes, but her version of the literary life was so Left Bank; even now, on a cane and weighted down with her immense turban, she staggered off to the Goncourt reception at Gallimard ("It was like the reception of the Princesse de Guermantes, average age eighty," she said dryly, "but I promised I'd go"). Rising from her sickbed she would hurry off to the Fémina party and the one for the Médicis étranger, whereas even in good health Jack would never venture to such merely symbolic crushes. Maybe the French go to those things, he thought, because when they had a court they had to show up at even the most tedious receptions; it was the rite of entrée that acted as a gauge and proof of their social worth.

"No," he could hear her saying wearily if he proposed such an interpretation, for she began many, even most remarks with the word *no*. "It's not that. It's just that we've always gone to the Goncourt party," which was her way, wasn't it, of rephrasing what he'd just said.

She had a house in a fishing village on an island off the Atlantic coast down near La Rochelle and that's where they'd spent summer after summer, so unvarying that one might be fooled into believing one was

eternal or summer was or at least this house and its
garden were. They'd throw open the two sets of French
doors, program the CD player with operas and piano
sonatas, with discs of Cecilia Bartoli sounding baroque
and indignant or of the two-piano *Dolly Suite* by Fauré,
which was French music as charming, as gay and sad as
Marie-Hélène's own conversation.

There'd be a flurry of activity in the morning when
Marie-Hélène dashed off to the market on her bicycle
and came back with a leaking basket full of shucked
oysters on a bed of seaweed or of fresh anchovies she
would later clean and make into ceviche with green
peppercorns, olive oil and lemon juice. On the red tile
counter she'd create a still life with eggplants, roses as
red-black as clotting blood, stalks of celery with their
bubble-coated peppery-tasting leaves in water, a scat-
tering of champignons de Paris still blotched with
earth. And sunflowers—huge sunflowers looking like
beheaded kings wearing their crowns, and etched-glass
vases of sweet peas and nasturtiums.

The postwoman would arrive with three or four
books, the phone would ring so much the receiver
would jump in place like a frustrated toddler in a
playpen, a man came to replace the tiles that a storm
had dislodged from the roof, the cats would hiss at a
feline interloper and chase her off the property, the
piano duet would discourse to itself about a childhood
more wry and fanciful than the unnoticed bleakness of
Jack's own early years.

And then, after all the morning excitement died
down, Marie-Hélène and Jack would subside into their

wicker chaises longues in the garden and read and write. The day would stretch on and on, the noonday heat would fade into the impossibly sustained diminuendo of the cool afternoon and evening. God, a director on a budget, would stop using color film for the huge fig tree with its large genital-covering leaves and revert to a cheap, grainy black-and-white stock. Around six, which was still as bright as the July three o'clock in New York, they'd bicycle to the beach and drink their Fantas beside the ocean. As they walked through the sand they passed every thousand yards another Nazi pillbox, these massive concrete guardhouses sinking and tilting, covered with the graffiti of several generations, but the only structures of the thousand-year Reich that might actually endure into the next millennium.

On certain days a soft white fog filled the garden like a powder puff. The sea would suddenly feel immediately present—briny and cold—and Jack would look down as if to see snails emerging out of the dark black soil. As he biked around the village in his green hooded ciré he glanced at the seven-foot-tall hollyhocks sprouting up at random like drunk soldiers on disorganized guard duty. The cold damp air was heavy and melancholy with wood smoke.

After buying a baguette and the *Herald Tribune* he'd head back to Marie-Hélène's house, to the nearly anonymous high wall and the shiny wood door painted dark green. The door would swing open, triggering a bell, and there would be the *chai* on the left with the firewood stacked neatly, the coiled garden hose and sprinkler and the aluminum wine rack. Straight ahead, in the garage, were more bikes and the rakes and shovels. Behind the garage, and seen through an open door, was the White Garden where the sheets, which were at least the right color though too large and flapping to be flowers, were hung out to dry. The main garden, with its old roses and herb patch and flowering bushes, its plush lawn and green wrought iron round table stamped through in tiny whorls of holes, its walls of soft sandstone, was small but packed with incident, a miniature Japanese résumé of the universe. It lay like an adventure before the whitewashed uneventfulness of the house with its Cyclops eye, the *oeil de boeuf* giving onto the stairwell.

Inside there were two rooms downstairs and three upstairs (two bedrooms and a study). Every object had been chosen not because it was precious or inherently fascinating but because it "went"—it wore a halo of family associations or because, well, because it had always been there. Jack had noticed that if he bought a vase for the house that was too big, too resplendent, too glossy, it wasn't anywhere to be found the next year he visited; the exact tone of the house was impossible to recreate, probably because it enshrined, mainly, the familiar and followed no logic. If Marie-Hélène had the sofas recovered at great expense it was invariably in the same sun-faded blue canvas (didn't rare book dealers refer to paper wrappers that were "slightly sunned"?). Only the crisper white piping revealed the upholstery was new.

In the winter they would come down from Paris and build great fires in the salon and leave the oven on all day, making clafoutis or a cassoulet. They'd stretch out on their matching couches with matching copies of the new Ishiguro or the latest Antonia Fraser biography of a French tyrant and stop only to sip smoky lapsang souchong tea brewed in the studded black bronze pot and served in black handleless cups lined in lacqueur. "Do you think it's all the pianist's dream?" one of them might ask or, "Madame de Châtelet, wasn't she Voltaire's mistress? Some sort of brainiac, it seems."

Jack was capable of becoming very cross with her if she showed up for dinner an hour and a half late in Paris saying as she entered, holding her jeweled hands over her head as if to ward off his blows, "I know, I know, but you can't imagine how I rushed!" Or if she overtired herself and went all day without eating. Or he turned red with vexation when she took up smoking again after stopping for six months. She would complain about American puritanism and say that her French doctor had warned her against giving up tobacco definitively. "He said it would be a terrible shock to my system after a lifetime of smoking."

She had the usual French fear of drafts and like many of her compatriots she'd say, when January rolled around, "Everyone is very, very tired. Everyone I know is exhausted." Jack tried to explain that for an American a breeze was salutary and exhaustion was not a condition requiring a sustained regime of spa visiting and herbal treatments but rather a momentary inconvenience that one good night's sleep would put to rights.

She warned him against drinking ice water while eating a hot meal.

He felt that she was overmedicated, like most French people, and that she wasted her money on her private physical therapist (her "kiné") who visited her at home three times a week for half an hour of feathery finger-work and microscopic spine and neck adjustments. Her nearly undetectable pummelings were a bit like those test drum taps a percussionist bends down to hear when he pedals up a pitch change on the bass drum. Jack was just as virulent in denouncing the expensive home-opath who prescribed her endless sugar tablets to melt under her tongue to stave off chills and colds—or to address this nearly mythical problem of prolonged and general "exhaustion."

Fortunately his rants had no effect on her whatso-ever; she remained true to her Gallic health prejudices, which were surely no more irrational than American medical superstitions except he couldn't isolate what those were, so enmeshed was he in his own national culture.

Of course a friendship is not constructed out of shared beliefs and values but out of easy, almost uncon-scious routines and reflexes—the habits of a lifetime together, not the sharp disagreements of the moment. Even the same old arguments about the same old things (lateness, health, too many social engagements) can be the reassuring noise that invariably accompanies the familiar signal of friendly love.

Now she was ill, seriously ill, but she was smoking assiduously "for her nerves," eating too little since she feared the cortisone would bloat her, going out every night because we socialites are never tired. She seemed to be keeping two ledgers, contradictory and competing—one in which she was planning a trip to

Brazil next summer, the other in which she was holding an emergency meeting with her lawyer to rewrite her will. In one version of her life she was quitting her job as a literary scout for a publishing house after forty years of service; in the other she was planning to have the pounded earthen floor of the garage at the summer house finally laid with weathered old stones, each stone so expensive it seemed she was having to pay rent on the centuries needed to wear them down. And this major change she had planned for next spring.

She was his hold on France and Jack worried he'd forget his French if she died. He'd been speaking it with her for thirty years and she still corrected his mistakes in gender, idiom and the use of the subjunctive. They spoke French at least as often as English and she ignored the elephant in the room, his accent, not subject to amelioration at this late date, but concentrated on the little monkeys, on the smaller, more trainable faults of usage, which might yet be corrected.

She was a repository of quaint expressions, elegant antiquated periphrases, Old France turns of phrase. She didn't produce them unconsciously as a peasant might but with delectation as an antiquarian would—like a foreigner, in fact, since in some ways she, too, was a foreigner in all her languages. She was always asking Jack how he would translate into English one of these impossible French expressions, but it was a bit like handing him a huge black radish right out of the earth and expecting him to turn it into a hamburger. He never had a gift for translation and in any event her idioms were hoary and unique to France and the French.

He phoned her every day or every other day from New York that fall after her diagnosis and his return from his weeklong book promotion in Paris. He tried to be cheerful, gallant in her manner, though the pain she was going through made him miserable and he had to pretend to be interested in what she was talking about, in the new Robert Wilson play she'd seen or the 800-page Nazi novel an American had just written in French. He wanted to know about her health but he realized it could improve only for the instant before relapsing again. The other issues in her life—in *his* life!—seemed trivial by contrast, but only business-as-usual cultural chat could provide the illusion that she might get better, was already on the mend.

Her imminent death (if that's what he must prepare himself for) made him think of his own in an act of that selfish altruism, that reciprocal egotism that characterizes every friendship. What was happening to her might soon befall him. They had weathered so many storms together (her husband's death from a heart attack, the death of his own French lover from AIDS) that they'd become the Avanti, avanti! team. Now she was letting down her end, as if their lives were a heavy log they had both been carrying; if she dropped it then it would surely slide out of his hands as well.

HE plunged into a new hysteria of sex. He met a handsome married doctor in his thirties with thick chestnut hair and the pale, taut body of a mythical Irish warrior. The man wanted Jack to play his sadistic but loving father, an elaborate scenario that involved a rectal thermometer, three one-quart enema bags, paternal admonitions and even a severe spanking with an open hand. To have this magnificent pale man in his arms and this vulnerable, broken boy crying on his shoulder, whispering huskily into his ear and using the L-word—oh, that was strangely therapeutic, at once sexual and religious.

Another equally inventive "regular" was an airline steward who wanted Jack to put on lipstick and a skirt while sucking him. The steward watched "pussy porn" (a woman with one dick in her ass and another in her vagina) while Jack echoed her slutty, high-pitched moans. One day Jack's handsome auburn-haired "son" called and asked if he could drop in. Jack said sure but thought it was the steward who'd phoned. As he stood just inside the open door to his apartment, he was wearing a Copacabana scarf around his waist like a skirt; the instant he realized he'd mixed the two men up he tossed his scarf out of sight onto a chair and in a low, menacing voice greeted the "son" in his boxer shorts. It took only a moment for Jack to make the transition from trashy girl to irascible Dad.

He liked all this traffic and make-believe at odd hours. He rimmed a young cop in training for an hour in exchange for a hundred dollars and told him that when he got his uniform to come back for a longer and better-paid session. The police cadet had dabbed cologne all around his crotch, which remained so virile that it was like hanging a pearl necklace around a bulldog's neck. Jack took half a Viagra and fucked a forty-year-old who admired his books and wanted to tell his friends he'd been penetrated by the novelist; he used on the younger man some of the dialogue he'd worked out for his "son." The Viagra made the car lights when he walked the twenty blocks home flash a pale scary blue; he got a headache later and jerked off looking at the pussy porn. The men in the movie never touched each other but surely they could each feel through the thin wall of the woman's flesh the other man's penis ramming asshole or pussy. Did that excite them or was it just part of the job? Or did they derive their own pleasure from hers? From her groans and fluttering eyes and the long curtain of hair she kept pushing back out of her face to reveal her made-up eyes, her lips painted white, the small diamonds piercing her delicate ears and left nostril? Was it because he'd excluded women from his bed for the last ten years that other men wanted to be his bitch or wanted him to put on lipstick or look at heterosexuals on screen—was this the return of the repressed?

ONE day he went into the porn store on the corner to buy a new DVD for Seth. While he was in there he drifted to the booths in back, guarded by a tall bearded Sikh in a turban the color of oxblood. He saw a short young man, in his early twenties, with huge black eyes, full lips and an intelligent look full of curiosity—he had a bit of a swagger but in some ways he was just a kid with a smooth face and baby fat. He was staring intently at Jack out of his dark, long-lashed eyes—a look Jack seldom encountered these days. Why would anyone cruise his grandfather? Was he a hustler?

But all the New York hustlers now worked online and by cell phone; actual spontaneous encounters in the flesh had been eliminated, as if no one could bear the uncertainty anymore or the possibility of rejection. All the hustler bars had been closed. Nor did anyone want to stand on an icy corner in a T-shirt and Levi's jacket while the paired passing headlights picked at his body like chopsticks. The photographic portrait had become the only physical reality; erotic photographers available to do sexy pictures for clients' online profiles advertised in all the gay magazines. The pose or the camera angle made the penis look huge, as big as a pink bolster, and the shaved balls became big as glass buoys in a fisherman's net. As soon as one made contact with someone online he would flash back, "Stats? Pics?" Jack never bothered to reply since his disastrous statistics revealed an outsize waistline, a meaty, sagging chest and a body that outweighed by at least a hundred pounds anyone he would consider bedding. Sometimes he'd write, "My statistics are hopeless but the point is I would know how to worship YOUR body." A woman might have been intrigued by the idea of total devotion but few men were. Only on specialized websites such as Silverdaddies (for mature "Jovian" men and their Ganymedes) or at various www addresses designed for chubbies and their chasers or bears and their cubs would he consider transmitting a picture of himself or a physical description.

Now here was this youngster looking at him unsmilingly but with classical features that promised happiness—he was a boy out of Caravaggio but with better teeth. He could be a funny guy, too, a joker—that was obvious. Oh! Jack suddenly thought, recomputing the boy's height, his pure features, warm eyes, assertiveness that was friendly but far from innocent—oh! he's Italian!

Jack found a video booth that had an empty booth next to it. The idea was that so long as customers kept feeding the screen with dollar bills to watch various videos, straight or gay, sadistic or vanilla, no one would bother to notice the activity that might go on from one booth to the next. The wall between any two booths was of frosted glass that left an opening about six inches high at waist height. There was some complicated way of pushing a button and lighting the room so that the divider went from translucent to transparent, from milk to water, but Jack had never figured it out.

The Italian didn't seem to grasp the principle. He banged on Jack's door and Jack let him in. Within seconds Jack was going down on the large uncircumcised penis and running his hands over the little boy's body with its slight tummy and glossy pubes and hairless torso—and the Sikh was suddenly pounding on the door and saying loudly, "No two people, no two people!" and Jack said to the boy in his very approximate Italian, "Don't preoccupy yourself, I live just fifty meters from here."

"Va bene," the boy said seriously, nodding at the total zany reasonableness of it all. Outside on the street he unlocked his bicycle and walked alongside Jack, who asked him if he was a tourist.

"Yes," he said in Italian with a huge smile, "I've only been here two weeks. I'm Giuseppe," and they shook hands vigorously.

"I'm going to give you fifty dollars," Jack said, "and I'll give you the same every time you come back."

Jack was just ever so slightly worried that the boy might be a thief; if he promised him money in the future he might behave himself now.

"I just want to make sure you keep coming back," Jack said pleasantly.

Again Giuseppe nodded as if nothing could be more normal or expected.

In the elevator Jack suddenly remembered that the young Filipina cleaning woman was in his apartment.

"Okay," Giuseppe said, shrugging, "that's okay. We'll make love, all three of us."

Jack was shocked. "We'll tell her we have some business to discuss in the bedroom. She's used to my ways."

In fact after Giuseppe left, the maid, Serafina, said, "Boss Jack, he's cute! You get all the cute boys! I call him Mr. Sexy. But Seth—" she couldn't say the *th* and called him "Set"—"is still my favorite."

"Mine too," Jack said. "He's definitely my favorite."

It was always the lighter-haired ones that she liked, too.

Seth spent the night a few days later and the next morning Jack, still in bed, heard Serafina telling him, "Set, you are Boss Jack's favorite! He likes you more than all the boys, even more than Mr. Sexy. You my favorite, too."

"But you have a lover, Serafina."

"He too old!" she said, giggling. "I want a young one like you. You look like movie star."

The next time she saw Giuseppe she called him Mr. Sexy. Giuseppe went into the bathroom to masturbate to keep himself from embracing her. His English was nonexistent and hers very sketchy; suddenly the whole apartment felt very Catholic and colonial to Jack in the nicest way possible.

Giuseppe kept coming back. He was intrigued that Jack was a writer and Jack gave him an Italian translation of a biography he'd written about a master criminal. Giuseppe read twenty pages and decided to write his own memoirs.

Jack raised his payments to a hundred dollars though Giuseppe feebly protested, "*Dai*, Jacko, it's not fair, I like sex with you, I don't like boys my own age, young boys, no, they make me feel too much pressure, I like women, older women, some young ones, and older men." Here he winked and said, "Especially if they obey me."

Giuseppe explained that he never really sought out men except for money. His own preference was definitely for women.

Jack didn't feel the least bit possessive of Giuseppe. He enjoyed their evenings together and took him to the movies. "I have no idea what they're saying," Giuseppe remarked, "but I think I follow it better than you do because I read their faces and gestures. I'm very shrewd" (he used the Italian word *furbo* and with his thumb drew a scar from his eye down to the edge of his mouth, the Italian gesture for paying sharp attention). Jack realized that he'd never gone to the movies or even to dinner with Seth; Giuseppe, on the other hand, was not afraid to be seen with him.

When Giuseppe started writing his memoirs longhand and in Italian, Jack said, "My friends make fun of me for never asking questions. What's your story, Giuseppe? What's your life been like?"

They were having dinner in a good neighborhood restaurant run by a distinguished, soft-spoken Venetian, who came to the table and told Giuseppe all the specials—a great long list of them—in Italian.

"Do you really want to know my story?" the young man asked, though calling Giuseppe a "young man" instead of a "boy" was just a concession to heterosexual prejudice. Heterosexuals thought calling a twenty-two-year-old a "boy" was smarmy. But in the eyes of any gay man Giuseppe was obviously one hundred percent boy.

"Yes, I really want to know."

"My father is a Sicilian gangster who's been in prison many times. I first saw him dragged off in handcuffs when I was five. My mother is Sardinian and her mother was widowed young and left with five children she couldn't feed. She put all five in an orphanage and I think that was a shock for my mother. She has no feelings—she's a very cold woman. On the other hand, she had to work two jobs to support all three of us children. When she came to pick me up after school she was never nicely made up and well dressed like the other mothers; she was always in pants and I was ashamed."

"The poor woman," Jack said—"la poverina," which was easier to say without irony in Italian, a language that, at least for a foreigner, lent itself to strong feelings. All these Anglo-Saxon ideas about hearty Italian peasants, about the operatic flash of true, uncomplicated sentiment were patently false; Henry James had already spotted the same silly preconceptions in himself. One day he saw a young man with his coat slung over his shoulder. "He sang as he came," James wrote. "The spectacle, generally, was operatic ... I said to myself that in Italy accident was always romantic."

But then James started to talk to the young man, who turned out to be "unhappy, underfed, unemployed," an angry communist who "would willingly lend a hand to chop off the heads of the king and the royal family." Suddenly James saw how wrong he'd been to find in the youngster a picturesque emblem of "sensualist optimism."

Jack told this story to Giuseppe, who said, "Listen, Jacko, when I was in prison one of the guards who was like an older brother noticed that I was always singing and he said, 'Giuseppe, the bird in the cage sings all the time, either from joy or rage.'"

"Prison?" Jack asked.

"Yes, I grew up in Milano. I was always a naughty kid, hyperactive, and could never settle down long enough to study. I was small for my age. The older boys in the *oratorio*"—Jack didn't know what an *oratorio* was—"all wanted to have sex with my older sister, she's that beautiful. She just laughed at them and in revenge they would beat me up. I started wearing long-sleeved shirts and long pants to hide the bruises, but my father, on one of his rare visits home, noticed my bruises, forced me to say who'd done it. He rushed off to the *oratorio* and beat up all my enemies. I said, 'Thanks, Papa, now I'll never be able to go back to school.' I dropped out, ran away from home, started eating out of garbage cans. I became a prostitute, then fell in with an Arab drug dealer. Soon I was so hooked on cocaine that I was desperate. The Arab had turned me into a sex slave."

When Jack raised a knowing eyebrow, Giuseppe protested, "No, no, I never liked that! I was just twelve."

He went on to say that before long he was holding people up to get money for drugs. "I was arrested when I was fourteen and put in a juvenile detention center for sixteen months, though I was let out after fourteen months for good behavior."

"How terrible!"

"No," Giuseppe said, "I loved it. For the first time I had a roof over my head, my own room, food, even instruction. I learned how to be a pastry chef."

"Weren't you abused by the older boys?"

"Never. I was the toughest guy. They were all afraid of me. But I wasn't so tough that I didn't burst into tears every night."

"Were you homesick?"

"For *my* home? Never. . . . No, but I woke up one day and realized that all I'd thought about since I was twelve was drugs and how to get them. Now I was clean and I looked around and I asked myself, Where are my friends? My girlfriends? I don't have any girlfriends!"

Jack looked at his lap, embarrassed that he hadn't known that Giuseppe experienced the absence of women so profoundly. Giuseppe said that he became bulemic in prison—

(*Oh, no,* Jack groaned inwardly, *that was the only piece missing*)

—because he wanted to be gaunt in order to please women when he got out.

Jack laughed. "Fat as I am," he said, "women always fancy me. It's men who are so hard to please."

They didn't lapse into small talk, for Giuseppe had none. He was interested in the people he met through Jack, especially the women, but mainly to ascertain their sexual amiability, real or hoped-for. As they chatted on into the night Giuseppe told him that after he got out of prison he fell back into sniffing cocaine right away—and into the hands of the Arab dealer.

"And then the Arab was arrested and there was a trial" (*processo* in Italian had always sounded to Jack more like a continued operation than a single horrific examination by fire or water). "In Italy a trial goes on for years. At first I was willing to testify against him for child abuse since he'd started pimping me and fucking me when I was twelve. But then I regretted my decision. I knew that if he ever was sentenced his friends would wipe me out. In fact the next time I bought some cocaine from one of them I almost died."

"Really?" Jack asked in English.

"Yes, *rillieh*," Giuseppe said, then reverted to Italian, which he knew how to speak with the remarkable clarity of someone self-educated, perfect for foreigners. "It was laced with so many amphetamines I nearly died. I had to be hospitalized and even though I was put on a drip my heart thudded so hard I thought it would drill a hole through my chest. I made a bargain with God that if he let me live I'd never touch drugs again. And I never have."

Giuseppe then talked to Jack about God for some time, more than Jack would have tolerated if the language had been English and the speaker anyone less sincere or appealing.

For Giuseppe was appealing. He had a rich contralto laugh that would flow out of his mouth with artesian force if Jack tickled him or said something silly. Giuseppe was "homely" in the English sense of the word—domestic, comfortable. He'd sit around in his underwear (which Jack suspected was not meant to be provocative but to save his street clothes from wear and tear). He showed Jack how to make a classic tomato sauce for spaghetti, which took a good hour from start to finish.

But he was still a professional prostitute and his thoughts returned to sex on every occasion—for once Jack had met someone who was just as narrowly focused as he.

Most recently Giuseppe had been working in a male brothel in Amsterdam, one of the last (the others had been closed due to drugs violations). He liked it there because he was in out of the rain, he slept in a clean dormitory with twenty other boys, the client paid the house not him but he got sixty percent of the take (his share was almost fifty euros a john). "Jacko, I can do about three men a day, but even if I don't come I get exhausted just from the constant human contact, from the needs of all these men, and after the third client I go out for a walk, even in the cold rain, just to breathe and regain my solitude. Three or four times"—he stopped to calculate— "*four* times I've hired a female prostitute just to feel the tenderness of women. Not to fuck—" (he used the Italian word *scopare*, which also means "to sweep with a broom") "—because usually I've already fucked too much. But to touch women's skin and kiss and joke around. If I have the time I'll meet a girl in the club and just kiss her, which I like because it's cheaper and more sincere unless she's too drunk to know what she's doing."

Giuseppe—"Call me Joe," he'd learned to say to Americans, though Jack's educated friends preferred "Giuseppe"—moved in. He had only another week before his temporary visa ran out and he had to go back to Europe. He let Jack pay him every once in a while but most of the time he refused. "*Dai*," he'd say, which was the Italian equivalent of "Come on!" And he'd push the money aside. "Should I pay you for the use of the bed? For this bacon you keep cooking for me every morning, for the hot water?" He took Jack's hands and looked him in the eye. "I *like* sex, it's a necessary part of my life, two or three times a day and you're a little piggy—" ("maiolino") "—which is also what I like."

Jack got complicated, so much so that he went beyond his power to express himself in Italian and Giuseppe frowned with incomprehension. "Well," Jack said, "I was afraid that you might be sick of sex, all these older men groping you, and I like you so much, I'm so happy with your company, that if you want just to have a vacation—I couldn't bear for you to think you had to put out—"

Giuseppe put his small warm fingers on Jack's lips, looked at him with big reproachful eyes, then kissed him and reached a hand into Jack's pants and felt the hard-on that Jack's own "goodness" had generated. "Little piggy," Giuseppe said, and a moment later they were both falling about laughing. Working among the Dutch, Jack thought, must have taught him about the perverse ways in which Protestants stimulate themselves. And he was ashamed that even altruism had become a vice for him.

Jack thought a three-way with Seth would be exciting, though Giuseppe worried, as Italian men will, that Seth might try to touch his ass. "Setto," he said, his pronunciation of Seth's difficult name, "Setto e attivo o passivo?"

Jack explained that he, Jack, would suck both boys' dicks or that Giuseppe would fuck Jack while Jack sucked Seth.

It sort of worked, all three of them were sufficiently serious about sex to brush aside any embarrassment and get down to it. And each of them, perhaps for different reasons, was strong natured enough to play his sexual role with conviction; articulated irony and visible shoulder shrugging were for amateurs. Even though all three of them were writers (Seth was writing a play and poems, Giuseppe was well-launched on his memoirs), they kept their observations to themselves. Writers can be the best sex, because they are truth-tellers and imaginative; they can also be the worst sex, if they start proving how clever they are and how excruciatingly self-conscious. Maybe, Jack thought, tragic writers are good sex because they are fully invested in the moment, whereas comics are always bouncing around outside the event and commenting on it.

But with all the good will in the world it didn't really come off. Giuseppe could see that Jack loved Seth with an intensity he'd never feel for Giuseppe. As a result Giuseppe for the first time couldn't really get it up, which put him in a rage that he took out on Jack. Suddenly Seth became protective and made calming, hushing gestures toward Giuseppe, who laughed out of confusion. Later Seth said, "Is that kid always so rough? You didn't like that, did you, when he did that?" and he mimed what he meant.

It was strange that he was so close to both these guys that they told him all their secrets, though he was old enough to be their grandfather (maybe that's what reassured them). Equally odd was the dominant role he cast them into (and they both enjoyed playing) whereas they also took pleasure in asking him for his advice. Neither of them read his words, nor had any of their friends ever heard of him, but his reputation hung over them all like an expensive fragrance—not important in the great scheme of things but nevertheless a distinction of sorts among young people who craved something fixed, something that counted. Jack, disappointed by the failure of his career to take off or even to support him, took his own reputation less seriously than they did.

Perhaps these boys, who were both constantly roaming the Internet, understood the possibility of even a very minor fame, a hundred hits a month on a Web site, occasional mentions on three different MySpace pages, three hundred items on a Google Search. What did they call this diffuse but widespread and sustained reputation that was possible these days, that hung on for years—the "long tail" of a comet that had long since passed? Was it possible that celebrity culture of the old sort was disappearing and that Jack was being childish and, worse, out of date to complain about his sales, as if they were all living twenty or thirty years previously? Now only a dozen strictly literary names or artists' names or composers' names could command general recognition. Now several hundred or even thousand names of serious people in the arts would be circulating through the capillaries of the net—small but extensively interlinked and strangely eternal. Maybe the day was quickly approaching when there would be no more sales of books, when young people would feel that it was their right to have free and unlimited access to all CDs, DVDs and books, to all information, and record stores would close, the chains selling and renting DVDs shut down, and bookstores and publishers would be put out of business. Every writer or musician or filmmaker would post his work online free and would count himself lucky if a dozen people a month downloaded his work. The only thing left that could be sold would be entrance to a live performance. Writers would travel, constantly reading, like troubadours always on the move, just as rock bands even now lived from their tours and the limited-edition albums they might devise that offered signed artwork, previously unheard versions of their songs, printed interviews and snapshots of the sexy star with his shaved head and tattooed neck. Writers would collaborate with artists to put out special deluxe editions of their work, too, for rich collectors. In that way books would become one-of-a-kind art objects.

The artistic world was breaking back down into tribes of several members each, but thanks to the Net, each tribe was scattered across the five continents. They came out of their basements and windowless studios to see *their* writer or singer once every ten years when he whistlestopped through their community or college, trailing his long comet tail.

When he tried this idea out on Giuseppe, the boy said with his usual confidence and idealism, "Nonsense! People are more and more bored in front of their televisions, I look at my middle sister with her mouth hanging open, losing her last few brain cells, watching so-called action shows where people shoot each other. But more and more serious people, real people, are returning to books, the real roots of their inner life. Writers are going to become more and more famous—writers will become the saviors of the imagination."

To prove it he wrote it out in Italian and handed the paper to Jack:

Gli scrittori diventerano i salvatori dell' immaginazione.

Jack's imagination kept turning toward not salvation but ruin. Now his bills from Paris were coming in, but he couldn't help charging new 2(x)ist underwear for Giuseppe to his credit card; he still took taxis most days because he was always late. He told everyone he was poor, but the only result was that occasionally everyone went Dutch, though more often they simply chose cheaper restaurants where he could treat them. The minute his teaching paycheck came in he mailed it off to the bank, where it was instantly devoured. A

European producer was talking about making a film version of one of his books, someone else spoke of commissioning him to write a life of Flaubert. He could get a dollar a word for writing a long piece about Nijinsky for a ballet magazine. He woke up at four or five in the morning and rushed to the dining room table and started scribbling, but an hour later he was eating his third bowl of cereal and feeling drowsy.

An interviewer from an Oslo evening paper asked him with unsmiling respect to describe his typical working day, but the man was so formal and Jack's days were never the same except always chaotic that he opened his mouth twice and nothing came out but a bitter little laugh. The reporter passed discreetly on to his next question.

Freud had said the writer writes for money, fame and the love of beautiful women. If you eliminated money, reduced fame to notoriety and changed women to boys and love to friendship, Jack had already accomplished all the writer's goals. He wasn't famous but he was so old and such a fixture that the head librarian at Kent State University had told him they were very proud to have among their collections ten of Jack's love letters, written forty years earlier and addressed to a famous New York theater director—and Jack had no memory of the letters, the love or even the director, whom he'd admired but forgotten he'd ever known. He'd been rode hard and put up wet, as horse trainers said disapprovingly—that is he'd written so much and so fast and had always borrowed so hastily, even crudely, from his own untransformed life, that he had no idea where or whether he'd described any particular event or person—and he was never astonished when readers told him he was repeating himself. Cocteau had said a writer should never worry about using the same anecdote twice since readers never notice or remember a repetition; Jack agreed with Cocteau, with only a few embarrassing exceptions. Sometimes his sentences ran away with him and began to dictate their own truths—he'd said completely contradictory things about his mother on successive days, for instance. Both statements were more or less true, but these half-shades became startlingly emphatic colors only because it was easier to write declarations than nuances—and sentences, once awakened on the page, began to rattle and writhe in their own direction, dangerous and hissing and no longer submissive to meaning.

Giuseppe loved him. They laughed so hard when Giuseppe played the hypocritical gay priest on the make ("My son, think of this as the host you are about to receive on your tongue") and Jack played the penitent but horny twelve-year-old. When Jack became too blasphemous Giuseppe changed the game to teacher-pupil; Jack was the student who had to work hard to prove to his instructor that he deserved to be passed on to the next grade. Then they showered and without another word they both went back to work writing at either end of the dining room table, Giuseppe whispering as he read out loud his own words and corrected them, like a nun telling her rosary. Jack strove to tame his urges to cook or call friends or cruise on the computer. They spent so much time together that Seth sent an e-mail asking, "Is your Italian genius criminal keeping you well fucked? Or has he killed you yet? Should I be concerned?"

And then Giuseppe's visa ran out. He flew back to Amsterdam with five new pairs of underwear, new jeans and a velvet jacket and half his memoirs completed. Jack was trying to interest his young Italian-language publisher in Giuseppe's life and *Life*. The last night they spent together Giuseppe railed some more against women and Jack said, "Everything about you is original except this disgusting misogyny."

"Listen, Jack, I'll explain it all to you—the women I've known are thieves, whores really, they're all whores, they make their husbands work and they do nothing but spend and they put out just once a month maximum. I'll never marry. I'd be afraid of suffocating, but I might live with an independent woman, an architect!, who had a career, her own money, who was already launched," and with his small dimpled hand he mimed a rocket taking off.

Jack and Giuseppe had lived their monastic life (early to bed, early to rise, reading and writing, eating simple meals, and like monks fucking each other three times a day). Giuseppe didn't really like to kiss (too macho for that) but on their last night together they lay in bed brushing their lips back and forth and rubbing their noses together as Eskimos were said to do. "Baci, baci," Jack could hear Irmgard Seefried and Elizabeth Schwarzkopf singing in close harmony on an old bel canto record he'd listened to a thousand times as a boy. "Baci, baci," he said to Giuseppe, who called Jack his "tesoro" (treasure) and whom Jack called his "angelo" in a perfect parody of these old songs by Monteverdi or Carissimi, whose very name seemed to fit these oddly assorted lovebirds.

MARIE-HÉLÈNE and he spoke nearly every day. A book of her dead husband's designs for the theater was coming out and she was supervising the color reproductions, overseeing the layout, proofreading the text, which someone else had written. She was glad to erect this monument to his memory, especially since stage sets were as ephemeral as dress designs; both survived only in drawings and photos. Her homeopath and her "kiné" were both worried about how her kidneys and liver were standing up under the violent assault of the chemotherapy; their concern expressed itself in new concoctions of sugar pills and pink elixirs and new sessions of fluttering fingers. Every day Marie-Hélène made pronouncements on the latest Rinaldi (a novel—not so good), the new Claude Arnaud (philosophy—very good) as well as the latest Spanish thriller or the brilliant essay in the TLS by Alan Hollinghurst ("No," she said, beginning with her habitual negative, "Hollinghurst would be the greatest critic if he weren't already the greatest novelist. It's no accident that Henry James was both the best novelist and the best literary critic of the nineteenth century in English. It goes with the land")— she meant "territory," but often got those idioms wrong by just one word.

A full month after he'd given it, a two-hour-long French radio interview was finally broadcast in which Marie-Hélène had made a brief cameo appearance praising Jack's work and his gift for friendship. Now she left a long message on his machine, which he listened to in the dark after returning to New York from teaching: "It was marvelous. There you were and I was . . . together . . . and you were so *funny* . . . and I spoke but I don't know why I spoke so *slowly*, what's wrong with me? But I didn't sound stupid—and *you* were marvelous, so *witty* . . ." (she always hit the double-t in witty, which for her was an exotic Anglo specialty, nothing to do with the duller, less thrilling, more pedestrian French *spirituel*). "The interviewer obviously liked you, he laughed so hard, you're even better in French than in English— that's what your editor said too, he just called up and— oh, Jack, I felt so close to you, as if you had put an arm around me, avanti, avanti!"

Jack had had other friends who'd died (of AIDS in their case) and when all was over and the body had been cremated and the Fauré *Requiem* sung and the few possessions divvied up, inevitably the most intimate friends had realized with horror they had no recording of the *voice*. Pictures, yes, but no recordings. There was no danger of forgetting Marie-Hélène's distinctive low voice, but he thought of buying a new answering machine so that he could keep this recording forever on its digital chip.

Buy? Forever? Both words had begun to sound problematical.

In any case he could get a copy of the very radio show she was talking about.

He received a royalty check for old books from his agent to the tune of six hundred dollars and he applied

the sum to a plane ticket to Paris to see Marie-Hélène—
well it might be for the last time, heaven forbid.

Over dinner a new friend asked, "Do you keep an
apartment in Paris?" and Jack said, irritably, "I never
owned anything there. I could never convince a bank
to give me a loan. And I certainly wouldn't rent an
expensive apartment there and let it just sit empty most
of the year or try to find people to sublet it. I did that
for a year once and it was a disaster."

"Not even a little Parisian pied-à-terre?"

"Not even," Jack said in a cold rage he managed to
disguise.

"But you have that house, don't you, on the Atlantic
coast, the one you've written about a couple times?"

"That's my friend Marie-Hélène's house," he said
severely, "and now she's very ill."

"Oh," said his new friend, a bit thoughtlessly, "so
after sixteen years in France you have no foothold
there."

Jack said matter-of-factly, "I'm an out-of-sight, out-
of-mind kind of guy." He wasn't sure that was true. After
all he spent most of his time writing about other countries, other decades and about people who for the most
part were long since dead. At least half of his e-mails and
calls were in French. But right now he liked—he
needed—this tough, unsentimental version of himself.
And it was true that in some ways he was indifferent to
where he lived so long as it had a cultural life, good food
and a supply of available men.

He wondered what would happen if he couldn't pay
his mortgage and in another month the automatic

deduction would come up empty. A clever, money-wise friend of his told him he could refinance his apartment and get two hundred thousand dollars out of it, which he could invest, but that sounded dangerous and improbable to Jack who knew nothing about money and preferred to roll seamlessly along in the tumbril than to take flight—or take action of any sort. For the last three decades he'd lived right on the edge of ruin, but he'd always been able to write another high-paying article about a French model or couturier or sell the foreign rights to a book he'd written years ago.

He received the alumni newsletter from the conservative boarding school he'd been graduated from in 1958. In the class notes he learned that some of his agemates had died, seemingly of natural causes, that all of them had retired and most were devoting their time to golf, gardening and their grandchildren, the three G's of old age. One had been the biggest distributor of beer in Idaho; a girl he'd dated had run a guesthouse in North Carolina "at the height of the hospitality industry in the 80s" and had now retired to San Miguel de Allende and written a funny book about her life. Some were practitioners of transcendental meditation or reiki. Many of them were selling their big house in New England and "downsizing." They were moving to cottages in Maine or Martha's Vineyard more "appropriate to the elderly." Jack thought, They're all loaded, peaceful and maybe enlightened. Very few of them, he said to himself, have to contend with financial fear or sexual activity of any sort.

Now disaster was averted one more time when Wesleyan bought his latest letters and manuscripts for fifteen thousand dollars. He was able to pay off his credit card bills, invite eight friends out to dinner, purchase twenty new CDs and raise Seth back to a hundred and twenty dollars from the emergency level of a hundred.

He thought he was like one of those hacks from another century whose clothes were at the pawn shop and who had to keep scrawling pages in bed with ink-stained sleeves and broken quills under an open umbrella that diverted the water dripping down from the leaking ceiling, an author furiously dashing off a guide to all moral questions (mainly cribbed from Condorcet) or a universal zoology which, like Buffon's, divided all animals into two great categories: the useful and the useless.

He e-mailed everything he'd been writing about his life to Seth, who took two days to send a message back:

> Dear "Jack" (since that's what you want to be called),
>
> I got quite a few laughs out of your Chaos, and of course I recognized lots of things floating in the stew like carrots and potatoes and chunks of meat.
>
> All the sex talk, frankly, kind of disgusts me, especially when you talk about shit we've done. I totally don't think that stuff's anyone's business. Really, really, that shit seems sort of sketchy and I don't like the idea of opening the bedroom door and inviting everybody in from the street to watch you sucking my dick. But thanks for saying it's

big and I'm hot—guess I should be grateful for the publicity.

You really make yourself sound so . . . so *low* and so desperate, but you live an easy life, no hard physical labor for you, you've never had to be a waiter, that's obvious, though you know I don't complain. I even get turned on by all the running around, interacting with all the people, guys flirting with me right under their girlfriends' nose when I cater a wedding. It's fun, all the drunk young lord type guys from Yale asking me for my cell number! I guess they never met a big Mormon from Provo at their Racket Club or whatever.

You're just on the prowl like me. All the time. I went to one meeting of Sex and Love Anonymous last week, you know that twelve-step for guys addicted to dick or pussy, or just to having one shitty relationship after another. But after one meeting I said no way like, *dude*, I can't give up *sex*, man! You know me, I rub one out five times a day at least, that's what's tough about living with two other guys in a studio, no privacy. I whack off in the toilet, so I guess I can't get too worried about your—what do you call it?—*chaotic* sex life? That just makes you just one more Chelsea fag—*just kidding!*

You talk like you love me and I guess you do. I *loved* our trip to Greece. After a week back in New York I was homesick for the island, for Penelope and Penelope's cats, that great café down by the port, our trip to Santorini which was so awesome and which really is fuckin' Atlantis! Magical! I loved it when you hired the little Chinese guy to massage me while I was listening to the Guillemots. I loved it when you called me "The Big Mouse" and it's true I can't sleep and I'm always snacking at three in the morning and then at five again.

Yes! Yes, I want you to pay me for sex, yes! Every fuckin' time. First of all it's hot and if it turns you on (and I know it does) you can hand me the bills *while* you're sucking my dick. Yes! Yes I like it when you suck me because your teeth don't scrape me and you don't run out of energy like a lot of wannabe cocksuckers.

No, Jack, you're a great guy, one of my best friends, I like telling you everything and I know I fascinate you, partly because I'm such a friggin' ANIMAL, hee hee! Admit it, you wouldn't like me if I was skinny and soft-spoken and broody.

It's weird when you talk about hanging out with my friends because I've always felt bad that I've never introduced you to them. I was afraid you'd think I was ashamed of you and it would be kind of sketchy to bring you along to one of the coffee shops after a CMA meeting—I mean, you might look down your nose at these guys, though I'll tell you some of these guys are *hot* and you'd wanna be sniffing around their butts. But well, for me it would be pretty awkward and uncomfortable to mix you in with them. I know you're sort of hurt by the fact that I've never mentioned you on my Myspace page as one of my friends, but my real friends—Joe? Bob?—they know we're friends. I've talked about you to them.

For the longest time I thought you were part of this conspiracy to make a snuff film about me. Seriously! Okay, I know it sounds a little woo-hoo, but I am paranoid, okay? And honestly, you're not going to believe me, but I honestly think that when I was tweaking really bad some assholes were making movies of me. Only the other day a guy said, "Hey, Seth, I bet you were more fun when you were using and all spread eagle and taking loads." Fuckin' bastard, he was a *friend* of my sponsor; I mean can you take that on board? But see, doesn't that sound to you like he saw a movie of me, some video a guy shot when I was passed out? Okay, okay, at this point I can just see you rolling your eyes and thinking, Looney Tunes.

So where was I? I'm a big strapping healthy guy, twenty-eight years old. I think I should go back to school and finish my degree, not for *them*, but for myself. But for some reason I can't seem to *mobilize*. And then I think I should start acting again, but right away I get into a paranoid whirlpool of who knows what about me. Even as a little kid I worried so much about what my classmates would say about me that I wouldn't play with them at recess. I'd just sit someplace out of the way and in my mind replay our last class and what everyone said and did in real time. I was a good writer. All the teachers said so. And maybe that's what writing is, mental replay in "real time."

That's what I have to get back to, writing. This is the longest thing I've written in months including e-mails and stuff for my page. I need to get back to my journal. Ever since last May my living situation has been so unstable. I was with that straight couple in Astoria who broke up and gave up the apartment. I was on Fire Island all summer living in the Grove but waitering in the Pines, but that was weird because one of the housemates didn't like me. Now I'm back in the City but we're three in a studio—I know, excuses, excuses. I believe that my play is good but that it needs work.

You say your life is chaotic but you keep turning it out. I've met at least two guys— hold on, *one*—who's heard of you so you must be doing something right.

I can't say I like the way you hijacked so much of my life since that's *my* material, dude. And like, I get the idea that you think it's cute or something showing my general fucked-upness, my liking certain bands, and so when I read those parts I thought they really made me sound lame and teeny bopper. I could just imagine somebody going like, dude, get a grip. That part about me writing extra verses in the style of Thom Yorke, so what? You said yourself you used to do things like that when you were my age, just with Marcel Proust and Oscar Wilde. But you know how much my music means to me, it's so important and it's really personal. Sometimes that's all there is for me, y'know. I really think it helps keep me sane. "Jack," man, it *inspires* me.

I know you listen to classical music and you think that puts you right up there with the angels, but try this one on: how about listening to songs written now about now in your own language by guys who are having to live through all this same Iraq shit and whacked-out economy shit we're dealing with right now? You listen to Mozart composed centuries ago in German and there's no *urgency* to it, no *now*, and you're not going to go to a concert with Wolfgang Friggin' Mozart dripping sweat and jumping in place and tangoing with the microphone.

I'm not saying you're out of touch. You're too much of a vampire to be out of it. You need fresh blood every day. I'm no better, don't get me wrong. I have to hook up three or four times a day. I sort of thought Doug and I might actually become lovers and remember when I thought I wasn't ever going to let you suck my dick again 'cuz I was really going to try and make it work with Doug? Maybe someday I'll have a lover but I wonder what I mean, what you mean, when you talk about love?

Isn't love just a woman thing? I suppose a man can love another man, and I don't want to sound like a homophobe and say we can't, that we have such low self-esteem and dah-dah-dah. But then I think it's almost a fuckin' female conspiracy to make men fly right and dish out the dough for the old lady and brats and dah-dah-dah. (Sorry, but I know that you out of all the guys I know, you know what I mean and right now I'm not too good at finishing the old sentences!)

I guess you'll put this in your book, too. But, dude, you really are a vampire, you know. Wish for your sake I could turn this into what my high school English teacher (I did take honors English, believe it or not) called "an epiphany" but they always sound kind of fake to me. Just remember you're my pup!

"Seth"

Record Time

LONELINESS CAN BE A FULL STATE or an empty one, by which I mean that when I was thirteen in 1953 I usually felt forlorn but occasionally—especially in the presence of a work of art—triumphant. Most of the time, at school, on the bus, on the street, I thought I was embarrassingly conspicuous if I was alone. I was convinced everyone was burningly aware of my isolation, almost as though I were trapped in one of those sweating grinning embarrassment dreams. In the high school corridors, gliding from one class to another, grazing the walls, I didn't retreat into a comfortably grim resignation, waking up only when I was seated once again in the biology lab or in honor civics. No, I suffered and smiled and mentally debated whether I should try to walk along with that girl I knew from choir practice or join those guys from gym class, who weren't all that popular, after all. My loneliness was ready to sizzle and explode as it leapt from one electrode to another: high-voltage emptiness.

There was the amniotic sloth of a long bath or the agitated mindlessness of reading the back of the cereal box over and over or the sadsack squalor of sitting on the floor in the sunroom, listening to all the clocks ticking in an empty apartment.

But mainly, every day, there was the same sort of highly anxious inactivity I'd felt the previous summer looking for a part-time job, waiting in the reception room in a starched collar, hoping to catch the eye of my potential boss, wondering why my appointment had already been pushed back forty minutes, observing the hands of the wall clock millimetering toward five, closing time. That's the way I felt alone at school, as though I were ready at a moment's notice to go into action, smile, charm, display my wares—but until then forced to wait and hypothesize the worst.

The other kind of loneliness, the full, self-sufficient kind, never came on me with lightning suddenness but had to be slowly wooed. I'd bring records and scores home with me from the public library and behind my door, which I'd outfitted with a flimsy hook and latch, I'd listen to the old vinyl 78s with the gleaming outer-space black grooves and round burgundy labels printed in gold as though they were Ruritanian medals for bravery. I'd listen to Vincent D'Indy's Symphony on a French Mountain Air (I can't bear him anymore, now that I know he was an active, hate-driven antisemite) or all forty-eight records of Tristan and Isolde (the work of another antisemite, one whom I admire, alas). The Tristan records were in four matching leather-bound volumes that looked like snapshot albums. Most classical records were numbered so that a good pile could be stacked on the spindle, then flipped, though real connoisseurs were against stacking.

I'd worked three months at that summer job to earn the money necessary to buy a three-speed record player, which would accomodate the 78s borrowed from the library as well as the new 33¹/₃s and 45s I was buying at a dispiritingly slow rate. My very first record had been a 45 of Chet Baker playing "Imagination" on trumpet and singing in his high voice stunned by heroin into expressionless, girl-boy neutrality.

The speed had to be changed and the needle flipped when I went from 78s to the other speeds. If the records were battered, the scores were often pristine— I held in my hands a first American edition of Puccini's *Tosca* with its art nouveau cover design of the passionate Italian heroine all wasp waist, long gauzy gown, imploring hands and hornet's nest hair. I saw from the dates rubber-stamped on the orange card inserted into its own glued-in pocket that these scores had scarcely circulated in the last half-century. These cards made me realize how neglected and private and chancy was musical history. Just as I could check out the first English translations of Anatole France and Pierre Loti with their white leather bindings tooled in gold and braided flowers on the spine, in the same way I was in direct physical contact with these early musical scores of *Cavalleria Rusticana*, of Verdi's *Requiem*, of Massenet's *Thaïs*, of Wagner's *Lohengrin*, of Strauss's *Der Zigeunerbaron*. I was equally intimate with these scratched recordings of Lauritz Melchior (whom I'd heard sing a solo concert in Dallas when I was nine) of Jussi Björling (whom I'd seen, corsetted and tiny, flailing his arms on the stage of the Chicago Lyric

Opera as he sang Rodolfo in *Bohème*), even of
"Madame" Schumann-Heinck, whom my mother had
seen in some Texas cow palace during one of her innu-
merable farewell tours just after World War I.

I'd come home from school by way of the library,
my biceps aching from my burden of records, scores,
and books, and I'd barricade myself in my room. As the
Chicago night began to fall earlier and earlier each
December evening and the snow on my sill would melt
and refreeze, I took comfort in my room with the siz-
zling radiator, the chocolate brown walls, tan burlap
curtains, gleaming maple chest of drawers, comfortable
armchair and the old brass lamp from my earliest childhood, originally designed before my time as a gas lamp
but now rewired with its glass chimney still intact and
its luminosity still capable of being dialed down into
yellow dimness. I loved the coarse red wool blanket
with its big Hudson Bay dull satin label sewn into the
upper left-hand corner like a commemorative stamp
showing a moose and a canoe. I loved the pale celadon
green pots I'd bought in Chinatown, their raised designs
nearly effaced under heavy glazes, their wide cork tops
sealed shut with red wax that had to be chipped away to
reveal the candied ginger slices within, floating, slimy, in
a thick, dark sugar syrup. Now the ginger had long since
been eaten and the bowls washed clean but they were
still faintly redolent of their spicy, mysterious original
contents. I loved my seven bronze Chinese horses, which
were stored in a brown velvet box cut into exact
silhouettes into which the little statues could be wedged.
Each horse was different, head lowered in a gentle arc

to graze or thrown back to gallop, each weighty and cold in the hand. I loved my music boxes given to me one by one, Christmas after Christmas: the turning brass cylinder under glass plucking brass tines that played the Gounod waltz from Faust; the unpainted wood Swiss chalet with the mirrors for windows that played "Edelweiss"; the miniature grand piano; the revolving water mill. But I was less impressed by the look of each box than by the richness of its sound. The Gounod I liked the best since the sound wasn't tinny but resonant and the box, if I held it, throbbed in my hand with expensive precision.

I loved the smell of the boxes of tea I collected and scarcely ever drank—I'd inhale the dry, smoky perfume of the lapsang souchong leaves, the Christmassy clove and orange odor of the Constant Comment, the acrid smell of Japanese gunpowder green tea, not really like a tea at all but a kind of grass, or so I imagined. I loved the way the hard metal lids fit snugly into these square boxes and had to be pried open with the handle of a spoon. I loved sitting on the floor, my back propped against the bed as I turned the broad, smooth pages of the opera scores in which the original words were translated, very approximately, into the same number of English syllables so that one could sing along. I'd keep changing the stacks of 78s, some of them so badly gouged that I'd have to nudge the needle out of a deep crevass, others so worn down that my needle, itself not ideally sharp, would just slide over the bald surface in a split-second condensation of long minutes' worth of music.

But more often than not the records were still in

good shape, perhaps because they were so seldom checked out. Sometimes for extra protection they were even inserted into translucent envelopes that were then closed and tucked into heavy, yellowing paper sleeves. The early 1950s record jacket designs were rarely printed with more than two colors and were pert or jaunty—black musical notes zigzagging like bees around a mauve cutout of Wagner's head, surmounted with his baggy beret, or all of Respighi's *Fountains of Rome* picked out in yellow and pink dashes and dots as though they were birdcages soldered in Morse Code— or else the covers were just dumbly romantic (a huge red rose superimposed over a brown violin for Brahm's violin concerto).

I was alone with classical music, just as a reader was alone in the library or a museum-goer in those days was alone with paintings. Everyone else in America was listening to Perry Como and Dean Martin or looking at Arthur Godfrey's breakfast program on the flickering black-and-white television screen. American popular culture was cozy, queasily banal, pitched at everyone in the family—there was no Elvis yet, nothing tough or twangy or raunchy, just all these bland white people, the men in jackets, dark knit ties and white dress shirts, the women in fluffy skirts and long-sleeved sweaters, acting out cute little skits week after week on a hit parade show as they thought up new variations on story lines that might fit the unchanging lyrics of a song that lingered for months in the top ten. People twenty or twenty-five or thirty-five all looked and acted alike in their dress-up clothes as they cracked their cute jokes and simpered and skipped between giant cutouts of sunflowers or waved from the flimsy back platform of a papier-mâché train.

One day I discovered the collection of circulating art books at the library and came home with a volume of ukiyo-e prints introduced by a spirited, seductive text. I liked it that these prints recorded the look of famous Kabuki actors or courtesans in the "Floating World" of eighteenth- and nineteenth-century Edo, that no one in Japan had taken these woodcuts seriously until French painters had discovered them. I liked the refinement of tall ladies standing in a boat, opium pipe in hand, sailing past the strutwork supporting a bridge. I liked the intimacy of a beauty coquettishly blackening her teeth while her cloudy gray cat tiptoed over her makeup table. I liked the ecstasy of a monk in his hermitage, the paper wall thrown open, contemplating snow-capped Mt. Fuji reflected in a black lacquer-rimmed round mirror. The crevasses descending down from the snow cap looked like the lines radiating out from a toothless mouth. I especially liked the young lovers running on high wooden shoes through the visibly slanting morning rain, a faint smile on their lips, their slender bodies nearly interchangeable, the umbrella grasped in their joined hands . . .

It seems to me now that I had few judgments about music or paintings or poems and if works of art were difficult that didn't put me off. I worked my way through almost all the titles listed inside the paper dust jackets of the Modern Library. I'd figured out that these books were classics, and if my attention wandered while reading *Nostromo* I simply started again and concentrated harder. It was not up to me to declare Conrad a bore or to wonder how a professional writer could allow himself to use so many words such as "indescribable," "ineffable," and "unspeakable." Similarly I felt it necessary to know something about Vlaminck and Van Eyck, about Rembrandt and Cézanne, as though I were preparing for God's Great Quiz Show in the Sky rather than piecing together a sensibility.

When other people, older people, took a strong stand for or against a Sung vase or T. S. Eliot's "The Wasteland" or a Jackson Pollock "drip" painting ("Pure charlatanism!"), I was so impressed by their opinions that I immediately adopted them as my own and sometimes repeated them for years to come without always realizing they were internally inconsistent and needed to be reconciled. I was so ecstatic as I sprawled on the rough red Canadian blanket, dialled my brass lamp down to its dimmest wattage, listened to Flagstad's "Liebestod" in which a human body was sublimated into pure spirit, as I smelled the smoky tea leaves or brightened the light and looked at my Japanese lovers in the rain, each wearing a matching black cloth hat that formed a wimple under the inconsequential chin—so ecstatic that I didn't think to judge these experiences any more than a starving man turns up his nose at food. I didn't judge things, but I was delighted when other people did. In the Midwest of those days we didn't live in an opinion culture. I was so shocked that I laughed, scandalized, when other people said, "This Sung vase with its pale raised peonies and delicate craquelure is worth more than all of Michelangelo's sculptures," or "Eliot is a fussy old maid with his royalist politics and furled umbrella but he has brought all of world culture together into a fragmented collage—fragmented because all collages necessarily are fragmented, but wonderfully suggestive and systematic, finally."

I was thrilled by so many sleek, purring opinions, I, a self-invented Midwestern public-library intellectual who ate books and records and art reproductions the way other people ate meat and potatoes. My kind of art meal was always eaten alone, just as I improvised on the piano alone, and I had only rare contacts with other art consumers. My mother's friends who had all the quirky, nuanced opinions seemed to have drifted out from New York or Boston. Their take on my favorite authors and composers ("Wagner certainly has his longeurs and if he is the greatest composer we can only add, Alas, just as Gide sighed, Hélas, when he named Hugo the greatest poet") seemed to me almost sacrilegious, as though they were discussing sales figures for the relics and relic-derived products of a saint whom I actually believed in.

To judge a work of art depends on a certain fastidiousness, just as to taste a wine properly requires not being actually thirsty. But I was hungry and thirsty as well as a true believer in art's miracle-working properties. For me artists and writers and composers did not exist in time any more than general truths can be dated (later, of course, I learned that each epoch produces its own truths, but we didn't know that back then). When I was reminded of the age of a work of art (by the fresh look of the *Tosca* score, or by a story about Pollock's recent death in *Time*), I was disturbed, as when a headline-grabbing geologist claimed he could now confidently date the Flood and had even found the exact landing site of Noah's Ark. This intersection of the mythic and the temporal struck me as indecent. I myself was ageless, unformed, an ungendered eye and I, too, resisted definition.

I had never played with toys as a child. I'd improvised on the piano, I'd invented complicated scenarios for my puppets or for my imaginary friends and me, I'd wandered through nature, receptive as a nose and eyes on a stem, thunderstruck by the smell of the lilac bush next to the Congregational Church, awed by the glassy tranquillity of Lake Michigan as I waded into it on an August evening and stood there, white and stark as a single soprano note, and watched the raised waves radiate out from my slow steps.

Now, at age thirteen, guiltily, I dropped the latch on my bedroom door and played with toys. Not real toys, not store-bought toys, but my own invented toys. I organized triumphal marches on the red Canadian blanket between ranks of tea-box military tanks, noble processions of the seven bronze Chinese horses, of a pink jade bodhisattva and a soapstone Buddha, of giant floats of music boxes all playing at once while the hordes shouted their approval (a sound effect I provided with my whispered roars as I hovered over the whole scene, invisible and manipulative as God). Finally I donned the red blanket as a cloak and put on a recording of the Coronation Scene from *Boris* and made my royal entrance, imagining the rows of bearded, brocaded boyars. I heard the clangor of all Kiev's bells.

I thought to myself, This is what little kids go through, this total immersion into fantasy, this self-sufficient solitude, the good kind, the triumphant kind. I was ashamed but not so much that as the school day would draw to a close I wouldn't become excited by the thought that soon I'd be able to start playing again—not exactly with toys, but with my fetishes, whose ludic aspect had dawned on me only recently.

My favorite games were all about power, benign power, the same games I played outside in the snow by constructing ice palaces, a Forbidden City for my solitary empress, an Old Winter Palace for my ailing Tsarevitch. From the opera records I borrowed I'd learned all about Boris's coronation and the pharoah's triumphal march in *Aida* as well as about the people in *Turandot* wishing the Son of Heaven ten thousand years of life. I was so high-strung that Mimi's death—and especially Violetta's—could make me tremble all over and sob hysterically (I wasn't your basic baseball-playing, freckled little kid); what I preferred, what I found soothing, were royal processions, and if I'd been Queen of England I would have managed to "process" on a daily basis, my raised gloved hand describing small circles in the air.

ONE day I read in the paper that Greta Garbo's *Camille* would be showing at a remote movie theater. My mother agreed to drive me out there if I'd come home on the train by myself (she verified the times). In fact my mother indulged me in nearly all my whims. It was she who'd let me decorate my room as I'd wanted, who bought me my Chinese horses and my yearly music boxes and who'd driven me all the way down to the South Side that one time when I'd wanted to attend a Japanese Buddhist Church. When I pleaded to go to a military school camp (I'd just read biographies of Napoleon and Peter the Great and was suddenly attracted to power even in its less benign forms), she enrolled me in Culver Military Academy against her better judgment; halfway through the summer I was begging her to let me come home, which she even more reluctantly allowed me to do.

It was a spring night when I went to see *Camille* in that distant community—a town I couldn't name now and which I never saw again. It appeared to have been built all at once in the same manner in the 1920s or even earlier in what was even then a nostalgic style, with converted gas lamps, cobblestone streets, and half-timbered store fronts. The spring was not advanced enough to have produced any flowers beyond big gaudy sprays of forsythia.

It was raining and the cobblestones were as slick and even as dragon's scales. There was no one on the street. At last we found the movie, which was being shown in a narrow church, perhaps as a fundraiser. If so, the programming was a disaster, since the only other member of the audience was an old man seated two rows away on a folding wood chair.

But once *Camille* began I was absorbed. Not by the humble, scratchy black-and-white look of the thing (it was a bad print, but my borrowed 78s had taught me to overlook that); I was used to technicolor, even three-dimensional movies, and I'd never seen a vintage film before. Garbo's acting style would no doubt make kids laugh now, but I was used to melodrama from the operas I'd seen. Anyway, this was an exaggerated style but unlike anything I'd ever witnessed before. She could change in a second from a sadness as piercing, as physical, as light directed into the eyes of someone suffering from a massive migraine to a joy that shook her agitatedly as though her big, lovely face were as bright and faceted as her pendent earrings. In one scene she was sophisticated and skeptical, one eyebrow raised, and in the next tender as my mother when I was ill with a high fever. Her voice would go from a fife's excitement to the bagpipe drone of her grief, a grief that really was just like a migraine that requires drawn curtains and deepest solitude.

I didn't quite understand why she had to give up her lover. What had she done wrong? Wasn't she even, all things considered, too good for him? Nevertheless, I liked the idea of sacrifice in the abstract and hoped to make one soon. Her lover had a straight nose and oily black hair, but I disliked his long sideburns and thought his acting was as unconvincing as his morality was caddish. That didn't matter—after all, Jussi Björling had had all the allure of a waddling duck but he had sung with the clarion tones of a trumpet calling reveille.

I knew how the story turned out from *La Traviata*, the very first opera I'd ever seen, but this knowledge made my tears flow all the hotter as the end approached. When the lights came up the old man was snoring peacefully. No usher was in sight, although I could hear the operator in his projection booth rewinding the film. I pushed open the main church door. The rain had stopped but the bare, budding trees were still dripping and the sound of my lonely footsteps rang out.

I found the little suburban station easily enough. A sailor was also waiting for the train, playing a mouth-harp, quietly, to himself, as though he were rehearsing a speech, trying to get it by heart, or evoking a sentimental tune for his ears alone. I felt washed clean and faded almost to the point of transparency. I was very old and wise, not in need of a great love since I'd already had one, afraid that something might jostle my mood, which I wanted to carry without spilling all the way home. The night was conspiring graciously to help me—the deserted, dripping village with the gas lamps and cobblestones, the sailor with the mouth-harp, even the sight of forsythia blazing in the dark on the hillside next to the station.

The train came, just two cars long. The only other passenger was an old black woman, asleep and smiling, split shoes too small to contain her feet. The sailor kept playing and I looked at the few dim lights that suggested the depths of these old suburbs with their huge wood houses in which everyone was asleep.

Back in my room I drank a glass of cold Welch's grape juice in the dark and pretended it was wine. I opened my window and toasted the wet spring night, which didn't feel like the beginning of anything but the very last plucked note at the end of a long, soft, slow coda.

Give It Up for Billy

HAROLD'S LOVER TOM DIDN'T COME WITH him to Key West that winter. Tom thought the heterosexual snowbirds were too old in Key West and the younger gays who worked there year round were too stupid. Since South Beach had become the destination for A-list gays (celebrated decorators, real estate speculators, media moguls and their satellites—muscle builders and models), Key West had turned into a backwater for balding gay couples from Toledo, the sort who owned and operated their own neighborhood dry cleaners and whose foreheads burned easily in the semitropical sun. They immediately took up with a similar couple from Lubbock they'd just met. The foursome were happy to go on a glass-bottomed boat out to the reef or to play bridge at night back at their all-male compound where the only men under thirty worked behind the desk.

Harold didn't mind how dowdy Key West had become with its main street lined with Israeli-owned T-shirt shops, its commercialization of Papa Hemingway's bearded face on the coasters at Sloppy Joe's bar on Duval, or its conch train that puttered down shaded streets and informed the tourists in shorts and sun hats about the Hemingway House and his cats with six toes or about Truman's Little White House or the Audubon House. Harold accepted that the world was becoming a product to be consumed by the world's leading industry, mass tourism. He looked at Japanese tourists as models for us all. They didn't seek out private, authentic experiences while traveling, or so at least he imagined. They didn't claim to be the exception, to be solitary and romantic. They weren't a headache for their group leader. No, they were content to buy the best known, most easily recognized luxury brand names at airport shops and to take their photos of the Whaling Museum or the Eiffel Tower or the Oldest House from the exact spot the guide indicated.

Harold had been coming here for a few weeks every winter over the last twenty years and he'd seen Key West go from a rough town of drifters and trailer trash to an elegant stronghold with artistic pretensions, including an annual literary conference on themes such as "Nature Writing" or "Journaling" or "Fact or Fiction?" Property prices had gone up tenfold.

And he was no longer young and wouldn't figure on anybody's A or B list. He was sixty-three, in a few days to be sixty-four, and about to retire from the American History department of Princeton with a handsome teacher's union portfolio. He had an arthritic neck and cataracts he wanted to have removed as soon as they were a bit riper. Tom, his forty-five-year-old lover, worked for Johnson & Johnson in public relations. Tom ran several miles a day and had no wrinkles, possibly because he used Retin-A.

They had an extremely open, easygoing relationship. Their heterosexual friends—and almost all of their friends were heterosexual in Princeton—said they envied them their relaxed attitude toward each other's extramarital adventures. Actually the adventures were embarrassingly rare and the friends in reality found their non-possessiveness confusing since it seemed to mark yet another spot where there wasn't a perfect fit between homosexual and heterosexual couples. People liked homosexuals if they were a sort of fun house reflection of their own image. They didn't want them to be completely different.

What no one knew was that Harold and Tom had long since given up having sex with each other. It was as if their original friendship had flared up into sexuality and jealousy for a few years before subsiding back into mutual esteem. Harold wanted Tom to have fun, even sexual fun, so long as he didn't fall in love with someone else and leave him. He couldn't bear to live alone in Princeton. Recently Tom had begun to date a woman from his office, someone who did community relations, and she represented a more serious threat to their life together. Women played for keeps, Harold believed. He thought female seriousness was biological and had something to do with sperm being cheap and eggs dear, or was it to do with spreading a favorable mutation quickly through the species—but such theories always struck him as kitsch. He knew that straights took their lives more seriously than gays did, and straight women most of all.

Harold relaxed back into his old Key West routines. He rented a bike and went everywhere on it, even on cold nights and rainy days. Literary friends his age thought it absurd that he didn't rent a car and drive around in dignity as they did. They thought it ridiculous that he insisted on teetering around with his big po-po hanging out over the saddle, but Harold loved the boyhood associations of riding a bike, especially at night down the cat-busy lanes and under giant palms churning in the wind. Most of the time he was tired and a bit dazed, as if coming out from under a sedative, but when he was alert, as he was at midnight on his bike, he felt as he always had.

He'd looked forward to going back to Scooter's, the go-go bar, which in the past had been on the edge of town where Truman Avenue shaded into Highway 1. It had been a rowdy but innocent place where skinny, Florida blonds and small compact brunettes from Montreal came out on the tacky runway, one by one, in jeans and layered shirts. Each did two numbers, the first one clothed and the second stripped down to a G-string. The unseen announcer at the end would say, "Okay, fellas. Give it up for Ronnie," a locution Harold never had heard before; apparently it meant "Applaud Ronnie."

He found that there were more and more things he didn't know about. Almost all the guests on late-night talk shows he'd never heard of—pop singers or actors in TV series, which he didn't watch. He didn't follow sports and never knew the names of tennis players and football stars. He could identify most of the current and past names in American studies, of course, as well as many of the principal figures in American history. He was convinced he knew more about his period, Woodrow Wilson's America, than about George W. Bush's.

Scooter's had moved into town. The bar was now smaller and cleaner and better lit. Instead of putting on stage any kid blowing through town, it now had a small permanent cast of dancers, mostly non-English speakers: a big blond Estonian, an intensely black Senegalese with biceps as round as cannonballs, a wispy Czech, a sulky Spaniard, a smiling Macedonian. They would dance for twenty minutes on the two raised daises at the far end of the room, then jump up onto the bar and coax tips out of customers before working the room.

They'd dance standing up on the bar and customers would stick dollar bills in their gym socks, but after a while they'd crouch down, their legs spread wide, and let the older men touch their thighs and crotches. The tips were rarely more than a dollar or two, whereas at Teacher's, the heterosexual strip bar, the men handed out tens and twenties. Were gay men poorer or less competitive—or did they think it a waste to pay out a lot of money to a member of their own sex?

The seedy festive atmosphere of the old Scooter's was gone, with its tables and chairs gathered around the stage and the lights—red or white, strong or soft— which the boys had kicked on with their toes, like Marilyn Monroe in *Bus Stop*. They no longer had an overhead pipe to do pull-ups on. And gone was the cubbyhole separated from the room by glass beads where customers could have extra feels in the dark for twenty bucks: lap dancing, it was called.

Now the proximity of the heavy foot traffic up and down Duval, those herds of tourists grazing along, released from the big cruise ships, acted as an inhibiting presence on the men in the new Scooter's. The whole place was just too visible and few locals dared to drop in.

But it was better than nothing. In Princeton there were no go-go boys and in New York there were too many drag queens for Harold's taste and not much lap dancing. He admired transvestites—their courage, their art, their antic sense of fun—but they didn't turn him on. In Princeton, of course, for so many years the boys had been his students: superb, untouchable. Now that at last he was about to retire, he was the age of their grandfathers and unlikely to attract anyone. He sometimes fancied an older man, but they seldom looked his way. Almost no one looked his way.

Night after night Harold, after a dinner with elderly literary or scholarly friends, would bicycle down the nearly empty streets to Duval, which was always busy, and to Scooter's. Gay bars, straight bars, closing restaurants, a big disco, the Ripley's Believe-It-or-Not, the handsome spotlit façade of the Cuban Cultural Center, the slow passage of cruising cars and pickup trucks up and down the main drag, the clang-clang of bells rung by professional bicyclists conveying one or two passengers in open rickshaws—it was all exciting, an animated little world. Harold chained his bike to a lamppost, visited the outdoor ATM, and ambled into Scooter's. He liked the glow of naked young flesh under the spotlights, the smell of freshly poured beer, the pools of attention as men gathered around a dancer drifting like a big, showy camellia through the crowd. He liked to sit at the bar and look up at these kids with their powerful legs, sweat-drenched torsos, broad shoulders, and unfocused smiles.

Sometimes one of them would drip on him. They were nude and extravagant as hothouse flowers blooming above all these old men. In Italy he'd once seen rose bushes threaded through gnarled olive trees: that was the effect. The boys were more often than not bewitched by their own reflections, which they studied in the mirror with alternating smiles and frowns. As one would turn sideways and suck in his gut you could just hear him asking himself if he was really getting a beer belly as Tommy claimed.

The men, of course, had once been boys, too, but not boys like these, not usually. These men were chemical engineers or hotel managers or accountants: nerds. Two of them whom Harold had met were English and ran a bed-and-breakfast in Brighton. A few, no doubt, had been good-looking, but not in the way these dancers were. Back then very few men worked out—and almost no gays. These dancers had gym-built bodies, legs bowed with muscle, tiny waists giving it up to flaring torsos and wide shoulders, thick necks, cropped heads. "Give it up for Ronnie"—that was the phrase that kept ringing in his head for no good reason. These dancers were shaved, tattooed, bronzed, tinted; even their pubic hair, when they revealed a glimpse of it, was just a shaped, trimmed patch, cut to the quick to make their genitals look still bigger. Everything—sneakers or combat boots, thong or towel, nipple ring or diamond ear-bob—had been thought out, but even so they had a reckless, raucous assertiveness that came through their primping like a trumpet through a thicket of quivering strings. Most of them were straight and spent the dollars they earned on local girls. He'd seen them stumbling out of the Hog's Breath Saloon with girls.

Harold liked them all, all of the boys, and when one of them strolled around the room in a gold G-string and gathered a group of old men (hands liver-spotted, backs twisted, mouths radiant with new teeth), Harold couldn't help but picture *Susannah and the Elders* by—was it Titian? That beautiful naked girl emerging from her bath, her flesh coveted by all the old men peeking through the bushes. Roses threaded through the olive branches.

IT took two or three days for Harold to decide he liked Billy the most. Billy was about five-foot-ten and he had a splash of peroxided hair, though in recent years peroxide no longer signified "cheap." Now it read "punk" or just "young"—nothing clear, in any case. Billy had a knowing smile and a faint scar that traversed his nose. Just a seam, really. A ghost of asymmetry. He had a solemn, level gaze, something serious and noncommittal but friendly about his manner. He had what personal ads on gay Internet called a "six-pack stomach."

He also had an immense uncut penis that once or twice a night he worked up and gave quick glimpses of. Sometimes, when he danced on a dais, he pulled his shorts open and looked down at his penis, which he could see but the audience couldn't. He'd mime the sound, "Wow," and bug his eyes, as if he'd never seen it before. But he went lightly on the comedy. He wasn't a camp. He was a serious, virile man but not forbidding, certainly not unapproachable. A man's man, who treated customers as if they were almost pals, though he definitely maintained a professional distance.

Harold gave him five-dollar tips and never groped him. Sometimes Harold said friendly, noncommittal things, like, "The air conditioner's on the blink tonight?" or, "Where'd they get *this* music?" After four or five days Billy would come over to Harold on his break. If Harold was seated at the bar, Billy would lean against him, throw a hot, heavy arm around his shoulders. "That guy over there," Harold would say, "was sure pawing you."

Billy said, "These guys must think we're really naïve. Man . . . That guy said he'd just bought a mansion quote-unquote in Key West and had decided he wanted to spend the rest of his life with me. He said he was a multimillionaire quote-unquote and would leave me well provided for. He'd take me away from all this." Billy opened a hand, then let it fall to his side.

"Jesus . . ." Harold muttered with feigned disgust at the guy's chutzpah. But why not? If the guy were alone, not long for this world, rich enough to feather his last nest with a nice gigolo, why not buy a young man who looked thirty and seemed unusually solid?

"I said to him, Why not tip me a few dollars right now if you're so rich, but the cheap bastard never parted with a penny."

"Hey, Billy," Harold said, wrapping a hand around his tight little waist, "where are you from anyway, Australia?"

"Zimbabwe."

"Oh."

"Do you see—"

"Yes I see. Former Rhodesia."

"You'd be amazed how many Americans think it's next to Tibet."

"Hopeless . . ." Harold groaned.

Billy had a polite, deferential manner, an impenetrable but friendly regard, a deep reserve. He might throw his arm over Harold's shoulder but it all felt like a professional engagement; Harold could almost hear the meter ticking.

A very tall blond man in his late thirties wearing a raspberry-colored polo shirt, pleated khakis and gold-bitted loafers signaled Billy, who excused himself. Harold didn't want to stare but he saw the seated man draw Billy down onto one leg and idly stroke his hairless, oiled thigh. There was no lust in it, just intimacy, and the man spoke rapidly, even in a businesslike way, while Billy nodded agreement. They could have been two spies exchanging information while pretending to be dancer and client. In five minutes the conference was over and the man had elbowed his way out of the bar, uninterested in the other dancers, though he did shake hands with the bouncer at the door and even spared him a smile.

The next day Harold watched a porno film his landlord lent him; the eventless subplot was about twins from Hungary, identical down to the tiniest mole on the right forearm or the small, cantilevered buttocks or the overlapping incisors. They seemed happiest when stepping off each other's joined hands and doing a back flip into the pool and the most embarrassed when they had to kiss, and fondle each other's smallish identical erection with an identical hand. They had identical ponytails. The main story was unrelated, all about a superb, dark-haired boy with flawless skin who so enjoyed being penetrated by a blond Dracula that he begged the monster to bite his neck—a declaration so miraculously romantic that Dracula was turned back into an ordinary human being. And saved. From what? Harold wondered. Eternal life? Eternal youth?

Harold worried about dying. He had de-dramatized every moment in his life, giggled at the over-the-top romantic scenes in a movie, accepted his mother's death with equanimity, even indifference, though when he'd won a scholarly prize for his book on Wilson at Versailles, he'd wept, since his mother wasn't alive to enjoy his moment of glory. Egotism, he'd told himself. Egotistical foolishness.

Life at Princeton—the university and the town— was so unchanging that he couldn't remember many key dates in his life there other than his five sabbatical years and the beginnings and ends of his three previous affairs.

He couldn't quite figure it out, but it was as if he'd worked out a strategy that if he didn't bear down too hard on his life it would leave such a faint mark it wouldn't—what? count? be noticed? Go through the carbon onto a master copy? He'd almost never been alone. He'd always had a live-in companion, although in the '60s he had still had to pretend that Jack, the man of the moment, was just rooming in his spare bedroom. By the mid-'70s the mores had so changed that he and Jack had been invited everywhere as a couple.

There had been so few ripples in his life. He'd produced only three books, but two were significant and still in print. He'd inched his way up the ladder to tenure and a full professorship. He'd had three or four star students who were now distinguished Americanists. One was even contemplating early retirement.

He felt he'd somehow slipped through. He'd not had to serve in Vietnam, at first because he'd been in graduate school and then because his asthma had been so crippling. Later, the disease had just gone away, even though central New Jersey was both polluted *and* saturated with pollen, the industrial Garden State. He'd been just a few years too old to become a hippie, and he was never tempted to drop out. He'd supported the student rebels in 1968, but no more so than did most of the other junior faculty. He'd come out when he was in his fifties, back in the 1980s, when gender studies had become trendy and he was able to renew his scholarly image by arguing in an oft-cited essay that World War I had been a forcing shed for modern gay identity. He'd exercised moderately, had never drunk to excess, he'd been afraid to try intravenous drugs, and he'd smoked marijuana just twice, both times with a Puerto Rican trick, and had felt nothing. Just when AIDS had become a real danger he'd met Tom, who was then in his early twenties and virtually a virgin. They'd been faithful for nearly a decade and by then had mastered safe sex techniques.

But he knew he wasn't going to slip past old age, sickness and death. No one did. He wasn't Dracula. He was considered practical and realistic and he'd take all the most rational steps toward the grave—or rather the crematorium. The other day he'd read in a new French novel, "He was accumulating as many experiences as possible so he'd feel less alone when he died," but Harold suspected the author of irony. It didn't work that way.

Harold knew that at best he had just twenty or twenty-five more years to live, which didn't sound very long. The previous twenty years had gone by so fast. Time was speeding up just as it was running out, like the last of the water draining from a sink.

Back in the early eighties Key West had been a good time-thickener because he'd known so few people and had done nothing but lie around and read. But now the island was so busy with elderly activity—luncheons, readings, cocktail parties, art openings—that the days sped by. Key West made Princeton seem tranquil by contrast.

Harold didn't tell Tom every detail about Billy during their daily phone calls but Tom certainly got the highlights. Tom had enough on his plate. Roger, their old wirehaired fox terrier, had become so ill with leukemia and in such pain from arthritis that Dr. Wilkins had put him to sleep.

Harold knew he was being irrational, but he thought they should have waited until he, Harold, could have said good-bye to the dog.

"Closure? Is that it?" Tom asked. "Everybody in America suddenly wants closure. Well, I wasn't worrying about your peace of mind, Harold."

A long silence set in. To change the subject Harold asked Tom about Liz.

"Her name is Beth. She's fine. How's Billy? When are you going to go to bed with him?"

"I'm not sure what my next move should be." Harold was grateful for this fake conversation to replace the real, painful one.

"Ask him over in the afternoon. If that man in the Gucci shoes is keeping him, the late afternoon may be the only time he's free."

"Don't you think it's odd he's from Zimbabwe?"

Tom laughed. "You don't keep up with the news but Zimbabwe is going through hell. The black president, Mugabwe, has encouraged roving bands of black ex-soldiers to kill the white settlers and expropriate their farms, and the soldiers know nothing about farming and the crop yields are diminishing and the World Bank or whatever won't extend them any more loans—it's a nightmare. As for gay life, the gay guide forbids readers to go there at all. The whole country is AYOR, at your own risk. People suspected of homosexuality are pushed off a cliff or is that Yemen? Anyway, it's *dire*, darling. Your little Billy has come to Key West to come out."

Harold said admiringly, "You always can orient yourself to a new person or situation within seconds. Whereas I feel like some sort of moral Mr. Magoo."

"That's right: I'm perfect," Tom said. He didn't take compliments well and was specially immune to Harold's,

which were too flowery and heartfelt for someone like
Tom, brought up on jokey, shrugging sitcom dialogue.

THAT night Harold invited Billy to drop by his place
the following afternoon for a drink.

"I don't drink."

"For a fruit juice."

"But not orange or grapefruit," Billy said. "They're
too acidic. Maybe an herbal tea would be best, or min-
eral water flat."

"What?"

"Non-sparkling. It's better for the digestion."

Although Harold found alimentary pedantry to be
tiresome, he welcomed it as a diversion from the real
question: Why should they get together at all?

"I can come by after my workout around four forty-
five or four-fifty," Billy said.

Despite the precision, he didn't show up until five-fif-
teen. He came speeding up in a red convertible with the
top down and the stereo blaring a Mariah Carey tape
(something Tom would have sniffed at). For Harold, who
liked no music after early Stravinsky, it was all the same
to him. The barbarians had broken through the gate, they
were the rulers, there was nothing more to worry about.

They sat outside on a little veranda surrounded by
shoulder-height bamboo walls. Harold had brought
back from the expensive supermarket cooked shrimp,
smoked mackerel bits, blue corn chips, and several kinds
of water—as much as he could carry in his bicycle basket
without losing control. Billy drank the water but didn't
touch the food.

When Harold asked Billy what were his plans in life, the young man said, "You know the tall guy who comes into the club to see me?"

"Yes. Who is he?"

"His name is Ed. He's an agent for models. He arranged for me to be in *Frisk*. Here, I brought you the February issue. It's in the car."

Harold had always imagined most of the readers of the "women's magazine" *Frisk* were gay men, closet cases who needed a heterosexual alibi in order to study other men's bodies. Maybe there were women readers, too. Certainly in this issue, he thought as he thumbed through it, there was a lean man in his fifties, a slightly flabby guy with a small penis and a beautiful face, and there was a photo essay titled "A Romantic Evening by the Fire," which showed a woman being undressed by an entirely depilated man. A hardcore gay magazine wouldn't have had any of these variations—the older man or the flab or the woman, but the guys would have had shaved bodies.

Billy's pictures made up the lead story. He was shown in various stages of undress, though the last spread revealed just how immense his "manhood" was, to use the language of the magazine. The text called him by a different name, Kevin, and said he was a corporate lawyer in Boston.

"So you want to be a model?"

"I'm already thirty and if I watch my diet and work out every day maybe I can stretch it out till I'm forty, but I'm saving every cent. Most of it I'm sending back to my Mum to install an electric fence around her house."

"Shouldn't you get her out of Zimbabwe altogether?"

"The cities aren't dangerous, not yet. She has a very nice house and servants. You can't believe how far the U.S. dollars I send her go. Anyway, she's running the family business."

"What is your family business?"

Billy looked at Harold in a penetrating way—frank, level, unsmiling. "Funeral parlor. My Mum and Dad emigrated from England to Rhodesia in the late sixties. They had a thriving business. When I was eighteen my Dad sent me back to London for a two-year course in embalming techniques, grief counseling, and funeral accountancy. Then he died and I took over the business. My Mum is the business manager. She's the one who has all the contacts in the community."

"Black as well?"

"About a third of our clients are black."

From the very beginning Harold had picked up on something . . . formal about Billy. When they were just standing around Billy lowered his head, let a noncommittal smile play over his lips. He hooked his hands behind his back and widened his stance like a soldier at ease. Now Harold could easily picture Billy in a white shirt, dark tie and dark suit, producing a white handkerchief for the sobbing widow.

Billy took Harold for a ride in his car out to another island. His cell rang and he laughed and murmured into it, but he wasn't speaking English. When he hung up, Harold asked, "Was that Afrikaans?"

"Zulu. Well, our kind of Zulu."

"Were you speaking to someone in Zimbabwe?"

"Yes, it was my mate Bob. Great guy. We always have a bit of a chinwag once a week."

"Is he black?"

"What? Oh. No. He's white."

"You speak Zulu to another white guy?"

"We go back and forth."

Harold thought it would be hard to maintain that a Zulu-speaking, African-born Zimbabwean was an outsider.

Whenever Harold asked something about politics in Zimbabwe, Billy maintained a low-key tone. *Sixty Minutes* had just done a frightening segment on the deterioration of the country. In one scene a group of armed black men in rags crossed a lush, well-tended field and approached a young white farmer. Their discussion seemed more a dispute over something like a parking ticket, heated but containable, but in another scene the charred, bloated dead bodies of other white settlers were shown.

Someone taped the program for Billy, who seemed shocked, silenced when he saw it. "I knew that young farmer. I *knew* him."

"The president was such an obvious hypocrite," Harold said. But Billy appeared to be way beyond outraged anger.

They had sex every afternoon. Harold paid him two hundred dollars a session. After a few days he suggested they lower the fee to a hundred-fifty dollars, but Billy was firm. "I need all I can get, Harold," he said.

Billy would appear around five in his red convertible outside Harold's gate. They'd sip some herbal tea and then move into the bedroom for a "massage." Harold would apply a thick cocoa butter with an oppressively sweet smell to Billy's back and shoulders, then to his muscular buttocks, finally to his calves and thighs.

Harold didn't really like massaging Billy's body, which felt too hard and unyielding. There was no mystery to it. It was like armor, not responsive flesh. Billy would talk in fits and starts, giving the news of the day, and Harold felt like his trainer. The problem was that Harold didn't really dote on other men, never had. He wasn't an idolater, though Billy was cut out to be an idol.

Decades and decades ago, back in the 1950s, Harold had been famous for his smooth skin; even the three women who had touched and held him had envied him his skin. He'd been lithe, small-sexed, boyish, though he'd dressed in chunky tweeds and worn wire-rims and seldom smiled with his thin lips. But for the handful of men who'd bothered to lift his fragile glasses off and liberate him from his heavy, thickening clothes, he'd been a *bijou*. Once when he'd been in Paris as a tourist he'd been picked up by a couturier who lived in Sartre's old apartment. The man, all sprouting whiskers and smoker's cough, had stood back, slightly amazed at the boyish genie he'd summoned up out of the drab clothes—"*Mais tu es un* bijou, *un petit bijou*," he'd said as he opened his hands, as if to bear witness.

Harold still felt a bit like that and half expected to amaze other men. On the phone his voice, apparently, sounded like a piping, eager, overeducated kid's, holding a laugh in, and young people who met him first on the phone warmed up to him, called him "Hal" and said funny, sly things to him.

After Harold had massaged Billy's back he tapped his ass, as a trainer might, with an unsuggestive touch, and Billy turned over.

There, suddenly, was the enormous uncircumcised penis, white and marbled and somehow *assembled*, like sausage meat. And Harold applied himself to it, as if this were just a customized kind of massage, given the shape of the body part. Billy kept his eyes closed and made not a sound until the actual moment of explosion, and even then Harold suspected it was less a sensual moan than a warning to back off in the interests of safe sex.

Harold invited Billy to his sixty-fourth birthday party on another island not far away. They all sprayed themselves against the clouds of mosquitoes and Harold's friends, a dozen of them, artists and writers and teachers in their fifties and sixties, were charmed by Billy, who stood about with his hands hooked behind him, his eyes lowered: the perfect mortician.

He was unassertive but friendly and open. He talked about Zimbabwe and his fears for his mother and sister. "I'm trying to raise a bit of money so that my sister can emigrate to Australia."

"We saw the *Sixty Minutes* show," someone murmured sympathetically.

"I knew that farmer. My sister has a beautiful farm, but she can never sell it now. I've got to get her out of there as soon as I can afford it. Every day counts."

Billy played with someone's four-year-old daughter and even laced an arm around the waist of a big-eyed, short-haired woman who'd divorced her husband recently, though the ex-husband was present if subdued. A man who wrote a column on labor problems for *The Nation* kept asking Billy questions about his job as a dancer. Billy smiled mildly; he had no hesitation in responding. Surely, Harold thought, he must be enjoying this freedom. He was never free in Africa.

One of the guests, a sculptor, invited them to his studio to pose for him. "I'm doing terra cotta figurines of lap dancers at Teacher's, women dancers and male customers, so I might as well do some gay pairs, if you're up to it. I don't know what will come of it, if anything."

They went to Sid's studio two days later, in the afternoon, at their usual hour. Sid paid Billy ten dollars for posing. By this time Harold's straight friends had all seen the issue of *Frisk* and they were all astonished by the size of Billy's penis. "But is that trick photography?"

"No," Harold said, lowering his eyes modestly.

Sid's wife said, "And he's a hell of a nice guy, too. He played with Annabelle's daughter for hours. I asked him to dance next month for our guests on Captain Bob's boat—we're giving a big party. Too bad you won't be here."

Harold enjoyed holding Billy's calves and staring up at him. Billy was wearing just a G-string, whereas Harold was in a shirt and slacks. Sid had rigged up a platform that simulated a bar. He kept pushing them closer together, not because he wanted intimacy. No, he just wanted to simplify their forms into a pyramid. Once again Harold thought of roses emerging out of a gnarled, twisted olive tree.

Harold dreaded their sex sessions. The rancid, sweet smell of the cocoa butter that Billy had brought with him that first time and left behind and that now had almost been used up. The lengthy massage of this nearly inert and unfeeling body and the sausage-making, which ended with a single groan. The ruinous expense, which Harold thought he couldn't reduce or eliminate, since it was going to save Billy's mother and sister. Harold couldn't even convince himself he was bringing any special pleasure to Billy, since Billy complained that Harold's teeth were too sharp and hurt him. Of course Harold had never faced such a big challenge before.

Suddenly it was over. The vacation had come to an end. Harold had given his straight friends in Key West something to deplore or admire, in any event to discuss. Did they suspect Harold was paying Billy—and so handsomely? Or did they think all the usual rules didn't apply to gay life and that young Susannahs gave freely, copiously of their charms to their Elders? He suspected his friends thought he was exploiting Billy, but in fact Billy was exploiting him, with his full complicity. Harold sympathized with Billy's family's plight and respected Billy's seriousness.

Billy drove him in the red convertible to the airport. He helped him with his luggage. They shook hands. For a moment Billy stood at ease, with his hands hooked behind him. Then he waved and speeded off.

Harold thought that his own decision to go on having sex at all was either a stubborn sign of the life force or a mere habit, depending on one's interpretation. He smeared Androgel on his body every morning, a clear salve containing androgens, the sex-drive hor-mone. Without it he'd never feel a twitch of desire. His doctor had prescribed it: "It'll give you some zest for life, improve your energy level. Appetite. Zest," he repeated.

Was he lacking in zest? For sex, yes. But for life?

Yes, he thought. Whereas Billy had a survivor's instincts. He was determined that he and his family would survive.

Harold was so happy to be back with Tom, though he missed the dog. Tom was dating his girlfriend three nights a week now. Beth. Her name was Beth.

A month after Harold came home, Tom said he was moving out.

"I'm going to try to make things work with Beth."

"Really?"

"You know how much I've always wanted children. A child. I only realized that after Roger died."

"What?"

"Roger was our child. But when he died I thought how pathetic it was to heap so much tenderness on a poor, short-lived, dumb animal. I'd like a human child. Beth wants one, too."

Harold didn't like Roger to be called "poor." He was so shaken that he didn't think much about Billy. Once or twice he showed Billy's spread in *Frisk* to his friends in Princeton. They said "Wow" but they were humoring him. They obviously felt sorry for him. Did they think he was to blame for Tom's change of heart, of life?

One day, while researching an article on Woodrow Wilson at Princeton, Harold came across a remark

Wilson had made twenty years later, after graduation. "Plenty of people offer me their friendship; but partly because I am reserved and shy, and partly because I am fastidious and have a narrow, uncatholic taste in friends, I reject the offer in almost every case—and then am dismayed to look about and see how few persons in the world stand near me and know me as I am."

Six months later he called Sid just to chat.

"Say, did you know Billy is getting married?" Sid asked.

"No," Harold said. "For immigration reasons?"

"Apparently it's a real romance. She's not even American. She's from South Africa." Sid downshifted. "I don't really get that, do you? Switch-hitting?" He didn't know about Tom and Beth. "You know Billy danced at our annual party. We took everybody on Captain Bob's boat and Billy was the entertainment. If I hadn't talked with him—I mean, he's such a thoughtful guy and then boom! There he was, bumping and grinding."

"Maybe Billy was never gay," Harold said. "Despite all appearances. I assumed he'd come to the States to enjoy sexual freedom, but now I think it was just to earn some quick money to relocate his family."

After he hung up, he threw some pumpkin-stuffed ravioli into boiling water. He was unaccountably hungry, in spite of the clammy summer day. A small, peevish voice somewhere inside of him said, "See? He was just using you and everyone else." But then Harold smiled, pleased at the simplifying form things had taken.

A Good Sport

I'M A RETIRED CLASSICS PROFESSOR seventy-one years old living on Naxos with an English woman friend, a journalist. Every simple statement invariably disguises several messy truths. For instance, you'd think that I must have been a Hellenist, but in fact in Ann Arbor I did Latin and can barely remember classical Greek, even though I studied Plato with Gerald Else, who tried to convince me to abandon the "stodgy, graceless" language of Rome for the "suave elegance" of the Athenians' tongue.

But I was a practical farm boy from just outside Holland, Michigan and I couldn't see how I could make my mark in such an overplowed field. Anyway, I liked the immoderation, the *perversity* of Catullus and Ovid's *Amores* and, of course, the *Satyricon*, but finally I specialized in Statius, who was relatively unexplored at the time I was coming up.

Everything was changing in the 1960s and enrollment in the classics was at an all-time low. But the cultural conservatives who wrote budgets and made decisions at Michigan State, where I started off as an assistant professor, were determined that Latin and Greek must still be offered amidst all the new courses on Maoism, feminism and Afro-American studies, as it was called then.

I snuck by, I published my dissertation, I rose to be a tenured associate professor at Bloomington, Indiana, but even in the relatively staid world of Statius I was gleefully able to glimpse the antics of the Emperor Tiberius, who at his palace on Capri would order little boys to swim naked between his legs and nibble him on the buttocks and thighs. Eventually (this whole summary bores even me), I wrote a second book, on Silver Age satirists, and ended up at the University of Chicago, which, paradoxically you might say, was too Socratic for me, too oriented toward the Great Books (in English translation) and Great Ideas endlessly debated by overconfident undergraduates with no sense of history.

Chicago, especially the Committee on Social Thought, wanted us to treat Caesar and St. Augustine, Terence and Cicero, as if they'd been writing just yesterday and as if they'd proposed views of the world we were all equally competent to embrace or reject. I'm someone who's never liked generalizations or conclusions. They make me nervous. I'd rather devote six months to a grammatical oddity such as a juicy example of hysteron proteron or hendiadys rather than a consideration of man's natural goodness, or to the theory that all new knowledge is the recovery of prior knowledge.

In any event, in retirement I ended up not in the countryside outside Florence or Rome, as you might have expected, but here on Naxos, where I can read the street signs and exchange greetings with the old Greeks (by "old" I mean my age) who live up here around us in the Kastro, the walled city the Venetians built when the island was still part of their empire.

"Venice" and "empire" might give the impression of grandeur, but in fact the buildings, which run into each other and are daubed with plaster and lime-washed white, look more like sandcastles than palaces. Every wall is on a slope (it's a devil to hang a picture true), every stair is slightly taller than the one below and slightly shorter than the one above, every twenty-foot-high beamed ceiling systematically rains plaster dust like dandruff, and once I'm up in my sleeping niche I can look out onto the kitchen through an arch that appears to have been *patted* into shape. If you study the arch carefully you can see fingerprints. In the winter when I'm up in my niche I feel like a kulak in a Russian novel gratefully sleeping on top of the oven.

The downstairs apartment of the house where I live has windows only at either end, so the inner two rooms are dark and cavernous, cool in summer and damp in the winter (one whole wall is wedged right into the hill beside it and is always showing patches of humidity).

My English friend, Helena, lives upstairs—and there again a simple fact might be misleading, for you might assume we're a couple, though I'm gay (non-practicing) and she's straight (non-practicing). The Greeks all assume we're married and it's convenient for us both to let that fiction stand.

Helena and I have known each other since 1981 or

so, when we met at the very *pensione* in Florence where Forster set *A Room With a View*. Now it's been entirely tarted up, no doubt, but back then it was a classic *pensione* with lots of British spinsters living there year-round and a ferocious landlady who charged extra for each bath you took. It was the whole slightly dismal world of shabby gentility, of retired teachers addicted to dog-eared Agatha Christie novels and visits to the Uffizi only in February when it was empty. The cynical, flirtatious Albanian waiter, who himself was getting long in the tooth but was, even so, thirty years younger than the average pensionnaire, would bring out each guest's wine bottle (the level of liquid carefully marked on the glass in grease pencil, the cork carefully half-inserted) and set it beside the used, egg-speckled napkin in a ring and the oval, plaited-fiber placemat, into which old toast crumbs were permanently wedged. Adnan kissed the old ladies' hands before and after dinner, having already been the recipient of several small legacies much contested by nieces back in Brighton. He ogled me as well, on the (generally safe) theory that all well-behaved American men on their own and past a certain age are homophile.

One day a deaf American biddy misunderstood Adnan's routine flattery and took it as a serious come-on, which she answered by looking him in the eye unsmilingly and whispering, "All right, then, come by my room at five, after my siesta, as we say in Italy." Well, dear, that's *not* what we say anywhere east of Madrid, and Adnan looked so small and alarmed that Helena and I fell about laughing as soon as we escaped and ran up and down the Lungarno. By suppertime we were joined at the hip. Both of us were there because of Forster—Helena because she was doing an article on Forster in Florence, and I because he was one of my favorite writers.

I'm not terribly sociable, though I'm no misanthrope either—which is to say I can afford to be highly selective in my companions because I don't at all mind ending up alone. I rather prefer it. I made the whole trip one spring break to Angkor Wat without exchanging a word with anyone but the tour guide and the desk clerk, ignoring the other members of our group, all half-gaga Golden-Agers determined to enthuse. My mind is like one of those big baskets rural grandmothers used to keep full of scraps of cloth and ribbon to amuse little girls before the era of commercial toys. I can just dip in at any moment and find odd associations, memories, imaginary dialogues, sexy scenes, translation problems, moments that make me wince and even a few that make me smile with a sense of quiet triumph.

But with Helena I found I shared an instant complicity. And she was as beautiful as a carving on the outer walls of the Miracoli Church in Venice, that small white marble chapel shaped oddly to fit onto a corner where two canals meet at an angle and a hump-back stone bridge leap-frogs behind. In low reliefs there are heavenly musicians in three-quarter profile tapping tambourines or breathing into a flute or opening their lips to sing, and the purity of their features, the precise carving of their nostrils and the philtrum below and the commissure of their lips, the way their long, smooth lids fit over their eyes (am I making all this up? Misremembering it?)—well, all that ideal beauty recalled Helena's at the time I met her. She had pierced ears freighted with delicate gold wires and gold oval frames holding translucent, carved bits of tourmaline and on her left wedding finger glowed a dark Bengali emerald.

Straight women sometimes assume that we gay men are indifferent to their beauty because we don't lust after it. Or they think we don't notice it unless we want to dress it or blow-dry it. But I've never wanted to be either a womanizer or a hairdresser, yet I can have my breath taken away by an old-fashioned Pietro Lombardi kind of beauty like Helena's.

She had only two or three conversational modes but I have no more and hers suited me. She could bark out orders with regal impatience. She could be full of mischief and covert satire, alert to pomposity or absurdity on every side but not cruel except to other women she perceived as rivals. She could curl up and be cozy while endlessly analyzing what some handsome man had said. "'See you later—' now what exactly did he mean when he added 'later'?" she demanded. "He was under no obligation to say 'later.' Or was he just being a tart like most men?"

And she might be airily dismissive of anything she deemed "pedantic," though as a good journalist she could swot up on almost any subject and she owned thousands of books, most of which she'd read and Post-It–noted. Sometimes during orgies of idleness she read nothing but whodunits, which she consumed in industrial quantities. For me reading has always been such a conscious fastidious activity (the Midwestern self-improver in me) that I was invariably puzzled when she'd pick up a Carl Hiassen and mutter, "Wonder if I've already read this one." Now I don't read much, except one novel on Istanbul, over and over.

We were very compatible from the start. She'd lived a big life in many countries and was good at languages. She knew all about court etiquette but scoffed at Americans drooling over titles—and our inability to get them right. She had lots of stories to tell, always new ones. She was usually on time, curious about my life but not prying, quick to roll her eyes if a conversation or guitar recital in the lovely ducal chapel went on too long.

We were famous for taking French leave (bolting without a good-bye, which the French consider an English failing, *filer à l'anglaise*).

She was fiercely opinionated and independent-minded in the best English upper middle-class way and was quick to dismiss an idea she disagreed with as "rubbish." I kept telling her to tone it down around Americans, who are notoriously thin-skinned and often only a step away from actual physical violence, but nothing could tame her. She was extraordinarily courageous. Once a dreadful man was telling us he'd refused to make love to Pamela (one of Helena's childhood friends, unbeknownst to him) because she'd been "mutilated" by breast surgery. Whereupon Helena said in a loud voice in front of everyone, "Funny, she said you tried but couldn't get it up—and that was before the surgery." She was fearless like that—and fierce in defending her pals.

We often took vacations together over the next twenty years. With her blond mane and *zaftig* beauty and elegant speech she was a male magnet, especially in the Caribbean, I recall, though I was the one who did slightly better in Morocco. We'd often wonder if a particular man would be one of hers or mine.

I'm small, well knit, with round gold-rimmed glasses, the perpetual half-smile of a little devil about to deliver the punch line. I have small, perfect teeth, small, carefully-manicured hands, a nearly hairless torso, high-arched size-seven feet which a big Welsh bear once kissed all night long with fetishistic insistence. Helena and I called him my *transi*, which in French means something like a bashful, passionate lover. He was my *transi*, and not the first. There was a Tokyo stockbroker with a wife and children and traces of a bad case of adolescent acne who turned out (much to his chagrin and my total indifference) to be Korean, heaven forfend. Once I knew the supposedly shameful truth of his origins he could never bear to see me again.

Then there was a Swiss-German conference interpreter, who could translate into and out of five languages at hour-long stretches; he was ten years younger than I but domineering and perfectionist; he worshipped me, and not just my feet, even though his passion took him by surprise, given his Nicaraguan wife and his usual preference for ethnic women or artsy, long-haired youths with gold ear hoops in their early twenties.

Many men adored me, which gave me a quiet feeling of satisfaction though I never paid it much attention. It's as if I never looked up from the chess game to see the fireworks.

For me the game was sometimes my scholarship, often my teaching, but most generally my own slightly smug pleasure in merely existing. I liked making myself little meals, doing yoga in a patch of sunlight, motoring up to Saugatuck, Michigan for a golden September weekend and renting a cottage there. Then, I liked rereading Evelyn Waugh or Ronald Firbank or E. M. Forster novels or bad French novels of the 1890s (I'm very good in French, it's my only modern language). Or thumbing through a new cookbook and turning down the corner of recipes I might want to try out some day (but never did). For a year or two I took up the harpsichord just so I could play Scarlatti's *Sonata K 24* and Couperin's "Les Barricades mystérieuses." For several years I toyed with doing a verse translation of some racy medieval Latin poems, homosexual doggerel written in the margins of holy missals by horny copyists, but then I reread my efforts and decided I wasn't gifted with words.

Into this china shop of a life Helena would come crashing from time to time. She found my way of living in Chicago intensely "boring," she said the one time she visited me there. "Next thing you'll be growing *violets!*" she cried. "Competitively! Good thing you like mumble-mumble ..."

"I like what?"

"Like being mumbled."

"Like being what?"

"Screwed!" she shouted, tossing back her great mane of blond hair and letting her fine eyes blaze before she crumpled into a puddle of hot-faced giggles, because she had a convent girl's love of shocking *and* a convent girl's penchant for wetting her knickers after she'd uttered a gross word. She was persuaded that only my sex drive saved me from total old-maidishness.

Three years ago, when I retired, I moved in here with Helena on Naxos, a lively enough island during the summer but rather dreary and underpopulated in the winter. Thank heavens for my Bulgarian friend Boris (though Helena hates him). Helena has a wonderful eye and has filled every room with old clocks that no longer work, little wood dressing tables painted pale blue, old sea chests draped in nineteenth-century embroideries from Crete, a great glowering sepia-tinted photograph of a heavy-lidded Cavafy, fine silk rugs emblazoned with the Byzantine tree of life that she brought back from Anatolia, mismatched water glasses and chipped old plates, all lovely and suggestive of a story. Her quarters upstairs are grander but messier (she's terribly messy if squeamishly clean—the washing machine never stops churning from dawn to dusk though the maid has to load and unload it since Helena is too fastidious to touch dirty clothes, even her own).

My quarters are both tidy and clean; I don't like even Eleni, the cleaning woman, to come in—she only disturbs things by dusting them. Helena has five cats, all of them with highfalutin names like Dido and Arete (which means "Virtue" in Greek). I have no cats, perhaps because I am one, tiptoeing gingerly through life or gathering myself into a glossy ball of indifference and self-sufficiency.

A Good Sport

I keep thinking I should have a project, but already three years have slipped by and I've done nothing useful, which infuriates Helena. She and I have taken endless car rides (she drives—the car is hers) and prospected every old Venetian tower or ruined monastery on the island but now we don't often leave the port town where we live unless it's to show the sights to American or English friends, who show up only in July or August. The first year, I escaped Naxos in January and flew to Key West, where I have two friends even older than I am, but the flight exhausted me with its change of planes in Athens and again in Miami. The second winter Helena and I traveled together through Morocco by rental car; she had an assignment from *The Telegraph* that paid for our luxury hotels. I receive a modest but adequate income from my savings and social security and teacher's pension (TIAA-CREF), but I don't like living close to the margin. We have an adorable doctor here but if I ever become seriously ill (which does happen to old people) I'd have to be flown to Athens and pay all the bills out of my own pocket since I'm not a Greek citizen and my medical insurance doesn't cover me here. Up till now everything in my life, but absolutely everything, has gone surprisingly well, though I recognize that now I'm on the slippery slope.

This winter I'm not traveling except in my head. It's February and a constant wild rain keeps lashing our five-hundred-year-old walls and here from the kitchen (I'm writing on the kitchen table) I can see and hear a shutter banging next door at the abandoned monastery, which is never used except in the summer when the church rents out very uncomfortable beds to Spartan Eastern European backpackers.

I've OD'd on reading and listening to my hundreds of CD's. Helena has gone into hibernation, or maybe she's just vexed with me. She has a terrible flu, which she's nursing with single-malt Scotch in a squalid heap on her big bed, weighted down by all five cats. She complains of the cold but says she can't bear central heating—so English. I'm quite happy with the hot-water system I had installed—I just flick a switch and moments later the whole vast domain is toasty and noisy with clanking pipes, a regular calypso band. And I keep a fire burning in the fireplace most days.

To fight the blues I do my daily calisthenics at nine in the morning, I bathe and dress with care at nine-thirty, I drink coffee and eat yogurt and a banana at ten, I check my e-mail at ten-thirty (usually just Viagra ads)—and then I have absolutely nothing to do and nowhere to go. If I'm feeling conscientious I try to memorize a Greek verb in all its many puzzling forms, but I find that at my age any kind of learning by rote is hard to master. But I must confess I haven't been very rigorous about anything recently. In fact not at all.

And then? Well, the days are very long and I've taken up the habit of daydreaming for hours on end and telling my memories the way a Catholic like Helena says the rosary. Aided by the exquisite black gum my Bulgarian friend has taught me how to smoke. Yes, it's opium but I'm too timid, basically, to become addicted though I do love the dreams it induces. And it's true that it releases one from all sexual longings, which you may be surprised to learn still beset me. My opium amuses me as does the old novel I'm rereading—*The Isle of Princes* by Hasan Ozbekhan, published in 1958, written in English but obviously by a Turk.

Why, just today I sank into an extended recollection of Istanbul, a memory prompted by staring at an old Ottoman ruby water glass, hand-painted with pale green glazed designs of foliage. I bought it in one of the little antique shops to be found at the very heart of the covered Grand Bazaar in Istanbul. After wandering through miles of kitchen equipment, cheap sandals, rolls of linoleum and racks of crudely stitched leather jackets (aubergine seems to be a favorite color), you finally get to a gate that when open admits one to a section that sells old Korans, nineteenth-century nargiles, pawned brooches and recycled rings, battered heavenly blue tiles from Iznik, dark carved furniture with tulip cut-outs.

Helena and I spent three months on Büyükada, one of the Princes Islands in the Sea of Marmara, and there I had one of the great romances of my life, a moment I keep coming back to in my thoughts as I look out at the world through my ruby glass. The opium helps me recreate the best moments but also dissolves the limits between remembering and wishing. I suppose Helena would say the whole adventure was just a pipe dream.

We'd happened to visit Büyükada three or four years after we'd met, about 1984, when the Turkish tourist bureau invited Helena and a companion (me, as it turned out), all expenses paid, for a ten-day visit. Our plane fares on Turkish Air, our hotel room at the Pera Palas

Hotel, our meals, our car and chauffeur, our wonderful guide Cansen (pronounced "Johnson")—everything was free. The idea was that with their weak currency the Turks couldn't afford ads in glossy foreign travel magazines but they could provide luxurious tours within the country to prominent foreign travel writers, with the understanding that such a boondoggle might eventually result in a favorable article in those very magazines from which their budget had excluded their ads.

Today Turkey is such a popular holiday destination that even Greece and Spain are suffering from the competition, but back then Westerners still feared rape, torture, imprisonment—all dire visions inspired by a popular movie of the time, *Midnight Express.* Of course the direness was not entirely exaggerated; once when I asked Cansen where I could buy some marijuana (I've always been partial to what the French call *stupéfiants*), she automatically clapped her wrists together in the universal symbol for arrest. Her eyes widened and she said or needed to do nothing more.

It was Cansen who took us out one day to Büyükada. Now there's a high-speed boat that gets you there from Galata in half an hour, but then there was only the sluggish little ferry from Eminönü, which dawdled over to the Asian side and the imposing train station built in the Edwardian era by the German Kaiser; then the boat pushed off for the four Princes Islands, calling on each one before it reached the largest, Büyükada, which means simply "big island." We were put up overnight by the government at a grand white wood summer hotel, the Splendid, with its red shutters, so striking against a backdrop of pine-covered hills.

Two-thirds of the island is planted with forests, the whole hilly interior, but the coasts are lined with magnificent wood mansions rambling down to the sea. A few of the houses are constructed in unpainted weathered wood, a sandy brown pale enough to show the grain, invariably carved into a carpenter's gothic, which strangely enough resembles the wood lace that covers old houses on Key West or Nantucket.

These are the "cottages" of rich people with their acres of showy gardens tended by dark-skinned blue-eyed Kurds. No cars are permitted on the island, just horses and carriages, and many day-trippers come over for a buggy ride (the "little tour" or the "big tour," the cuçuk-tura or the büyük-tura). Oh, there's nothing more peaceful or poetic than a clip-clop through the cool, dry forests as we glimpse the Sea of Marmara through the branches, everything smelling of resin baking in the sun. The pines turn brown under the intense sunlight, though you can say in favor of Istanbul weather that it changes every day, now cool and blowy, now hot and airless, now rainy, usually dry.

Once we stopped under the trees and out of nowhere a boy rose up like a genie with a big tin samovar and small green tea glasses. Suddenly we felt a bit like Rumi contemplating the rolling, darkening sea and sipping our heavily sugared tea (so sweet it attracted little bees) as we sat cross-legged on the slippery, redolent pine needles. We fell into a very pasha-like indolence, one that resembles those that are opiate-induced, a rich pleasure that absolutely requires the anxious attendance of onlooking servants. Just a hint of cruelty enhances any pleasure.

Our idyll lasted just a day. The next night we were back at the Pera Palas, rising slowly in the filigreed cage of an elevator (a hydraulic relic of the 1890s) to the small hot rooms under the eaves that the Turkish government had arranged for us.

We conferred. We had no choice. We *had* to find an apartment or house on that island, which was so unusual, so impossible to "place," that I was convinced it could be used as a surreal backdrop for a dreamlike film. When we happened to be there it was at the time of the Greater Bayram, the Festival of Sacrifice, which commemorates the ransom of Ishmael (or is it Isaac?), ram substituted for boy. On the streets of Istanbul I saw an elegant businessman at Eminönü in his tie, German eyeglasses, Oxford shirt, Italian shoes and three-piece suit leading a brightly dyed live sheep by a leash onto a waiting barge headed for Büyükada. The contrast (the city of course straddles Asia and Europe) struck me as telling and picturesque—no more folkloric than our own Easter egg hunts or Passion Plays, to be sure.

THE only problem about renting a place on Büyükada was that all the people who lived there were rich and had no need to let their flats, especially given that the season was short (no one except servants lived there in the winter). And it was a respectable place, reserved to married parents with children and no riotous habits. Even the resourceful Cansen came up empty-handed. Ordinarily when one asked her a question she had a

severe, almost curt way of grunting assent and nodding
minutely without ever blinking her huge eyes the color
of the sea on a cloudy day; the grunt and nod indicated, as in this case, that she'd taken in the request
without necessarily having figured out a way to grant
it. We were so eager this time, however, that we pressed
her. Then she seemed almost startled out of a trance,
shrugged her big shoulders under the heavy padding of
her Soviet-style bureaucratic suit jacket. "I really don't
know—but I'll sink." And she tapped her forehead
with her outstretched index and middle fingers to indicate serious "sinking."

Her thinking produced an invitation for a glass of
cold cherry juice on the shaded balcony of a Mrs. Tekinhan. We crossed the Bosphorus via the new Japanese-
built suspension bridge and drove through endlessly
proliferating brand-new slums of ten- and twelve-story
projects on the Asia side, streets without trees or lights or
even in some spots paving. At last we arrived at the
elegant old houses lining the Sea of Marmara. That's
where our hostess lived under blue and white striped
awnings. She was a trim, fifty-something woman with a
fine slim-hipped figure, her graying hair pulled back in
a severe bun decorated with a paper gardenia, her face
tan and lean with a large nose and a wen at the end of
one eyebrow. She reminded me of Maria Callas. She had
a low, musical voice and she moved us rapidly through
rooms that could have belonged to any bourgeois lady
on the Cap d'Antibes, save for the spindly brass tables
and a big creepy painting of turbaned officials with
white impassive moon-shaped faces beating a prisoner

with exactly the same face, all sporting the same pencil-thin mustache. Everything in her apartment was immaculate. I'm sure she had a maid or even several but they were nowhere to be seen.

It seemed she had a house to rent, a vast old wood *yali* as the nineteenth-century mansions were called. She and her husband were going to Switzerland in a week, to Arosa for a cure, and she saw no *major* reason against renting the *yali* to such a sympathetic couple, especially if we kept on the same servants—one of us was a scholar, no, and his wife a writer, no? Mrs. Tekinhan averred that she adored foreign intellectuals and counted many of them among her friends. She even knew a French academician named Jean-Louis Curtis, such a charmer, were we familiar with his delicious novels?

And then I saw him, the son, in a long white coat without a collar that buttoned down to his knees with small white irregular shell buttons, a shirt-coat that had been bleached and ironed to blinding perfection. He was twenty-eight or -nine, I guessed, not tall, his hair a glossy black cap, his body dark and slender inside its full white tunic, which at the time I assumed must be Turkish at-home mufti but that later I deduced was a summer garment of his own design. He had a canny, intelligent face. His shoulders were hunched slightly forward, which hollowed out his chest.

His mother glimpsed him too and called him to join us. His name was Davud.

I should mention that when I met Helena she sometimes annoyed me by mocking gay men. She acted as if we were sexual imbeciles who hadn't yet gotten the point of women. In talking about gays she was by turns too bawdy or obtuse or dismissive or pitying or just openly contemptuous. Once when I referred to an old college girlfriend of mine she croaked with laughter and said in her swoopiest voice, "You! With a woman! Why, you wouldn't know which end to approach. It *is* the front side usually—you do know that at least, I trust?" When I appeared irritated with the tone she was taking she said, "Men and women were built to fit together, tongue and groove, you will concede. Everything else you people do is just a form of groping. There have been men I would only grope. I'm not against groping—but it's not the tongue and groove God intended."

I teased her going on about tongues and about "divinely ordained cunnilingus." To be frank, I myself shift through many negative thoughts about homosexuals, but Helena's responses always seemed slapdash, condescending and out of synch with my own. I suppose you could say I'm hyper-discreet, the sort of closet queen the French call *une honteuse* (an "ashamed woman"), though I am by nature secretive and would have been just as elusive if I'd been straight (Helena has no idea how often my Bulgarian friend visits). And in the Third World, where I've worked most spectacularly as a "sexual operative," flamboyance in men is frowned on.

Or worse. Once when I was in Yemen as a tourist, four bare-chested Germans in tight leather shorts and sporting gold nipple rings roared into the town of Taiz on motorcycles. Within minutes all four were shot and killed (every Yemeni in that area carries a Kalishnikov).

It's best to play (what I actually am) the mild-mannered little professor with the friendly smile, a few words of polite Arabic, and an inexhaustible patience in debating the relative merits of Christianity and Islam (both of which, truth be told, I despise, though in seductive talks with earnest young *fedayeen* I always favor the Prophet).

So you can imagine how grating Helena's sneering could strike me. Luckily she is a diplomat's daughter and she quickly reformed. Perhaps she'd been a bit superior when we first met because she was much courted back then. In her favor it should be said she's always been an impulsive, generous friend, someone who might suddenly send you (me in this case) twenty-three antique lace pillowcases through the mail with a two-line note saying she was sharing them given what a sinful quantity she'd accumulated. Or she might mail an air ticket to London to a New York painter friend quietly starving to death on the Lower East Side.

That generosity co-existed initially with the conviction that she, as a desirable heterosexual woman, was a player while I, as a poor childish gay, was a mere onlooker at Belshazzar's Feast. She'd say, "Oh, Harold's not jealous of *you*. He likes it I have an amusing little capon." And then she'd reach out to touch my sleeve with an adorable pudgy hand and sing out, "I'm just teasing you!"

If I looked fussed she'd add in a softer contralto, "It's enough he has to put up with Langdon" (her husband). "He couldn't cope with another whole rival. Anyway, he said *cicerone*, not 'capon.' I said that, or the imp of the perverse did."

Her personal life was very messy; we were going to

write her memoirs and call it *Messy Loves*. Her older lover Colin was a rich man, someone who'd started out as a greengrocer and ended up as the proprietor of a small Elizabethan castle. Though he'd been born on the East End he'd acquired a posh accent and lots of first editions and some good pieces of Ch'ing porcelain. He was married to a stylish, bookish Italian called Concetta whom he refused to leave (she was a baronessa). When he became overnight through some adroit purchases a media giant and was himself under scrutiny he insisted Helena throw everyone off the scent by getting married. The only problem was that her designated new husband, Langdon, Colin's porcelain dealer, didn't grasp that their marriage was meant to be one of convenience, hers. And Colin's. Langdon wanted to consummate the *mariage blanc*. Helena was a good sport and sort of complied (maybe that's where she got her notions of "groping," for after all Langdon *was* her husband and he wasn't ugly), but when Colin discovered what was going on he was livid. Pretty comical if you think about it: the lover cuckolded by the husband.

Not so funny the way it all ended. *Spy* got hold of it and *The Sun*, then all the other—I won't say "tabloids" since every newspaper in the UK is a scandal sheet now, even the *Times*. Messy divorce, and then Baronessa Concetta was obliged to call her Harold to heel. Helena limped out of the ruins with a reputation; all those debutante tarts who publish their desultory little "diaries" in the papers called Helena to wheedle out of her a "tiny thought about adultery." Helena became very skilled at hanging up on people.

After that she had more affairs, of course, but if the man was rich or famous it got onto the third or fourth page ("Hopalong Helena Mounts Another Labor Lord"). Once the night watchman at a magazine where she was working freelance caught her "at it" as he elegantly put it and *ran*—I mean *ran*—to phone it in to *Spy*. Helena sued and won but never worked there again.

She fell asleep too early, put on weight, spent more time with her cats than with people. After six in the evening she was hopeless; she turned on the "wind machine," as we called it—she was always yawning and couldn't concentrate and talked to her cats even when her guests were saying something.

IT took a while but gradually Helena was giving up on London. She spent much of the year in Greece or the Caribbean or Southeast Asia churning out her articles. Of course her mother thought she was only inviting "disagreeable misadventures" by traveling to such places, but as Helena put it, "Cairo has a lower crime rate than Winterthur, Switzerland."

She sold her London flat and bought her vast ancient house on Naxos. But I should point out that her disappointment in love, the notoriety she'd acquired soured her on men, heterosexual men. She decided that sex—pure, exciting, unfeeling sex—she didn't much like except once every three years with a thrilling stranger. Otherwise, with steady beaux, she could tolerate the act only if it was accompanied by heaps and heaps of devotion and tenderness and build-up. Since fewer and fewer men were wooing her now, she hung up her gloves as a sexual contender. "I never miss it," she said. "I never even think about it. That chapter is closed. I lead an entirely virtuous life," she said half-humorously but with a serious intent. She went to mass every Sunday.

Until I became so close to Helena I never understood how fragile and romantic women are by nature. Very few men seem to fathom that essential difference between men and women, their fragility. Oddly, I think she's come to prefer my company and that of two other gay male friends, though they live in New York (they're Welsh but have worked in America for the last fifteen years). She doesn't see them often; me she sees every day, unless we're on the outs, as we are now.

She and I are well suited. I'm certainly not fragile, yet I'm a good deal more "civilized" if you will than most of the gay men of my generation. I've probably not slept with more than thirty men in my entire fifty years of sexual maturity. That may sound like a lot but believe me, some of these gays get up into the hundreds and even thousands. I don't like big muscles or strict role-playing or any sort of to-do about gay identity. I think private life should be private. A casual pickup does nothing for me. I've never marched in a gay parade and when the Rainbow Club at Bloomington invited me to be the gay faculty advisor I refused. I like mystery and subtlety. That must be why I prefer the bisexuals I find in out-of-the-way places to New York or San Francisco clones or circuit queens or ghetto ladies. Like Helena I enjoy being courted; the game of seduction, with all its false starts, dead ends and sudden rewards, is something I prize as much as the old bump-and-grind.

Helena and I are both good cooks and we both appreciate good wines.

"PERHAPS I can give you a tour of our *yali* on Büyükada," Davud was saying there under the striped awnings as we sipped our cherry juice.

Cansen grunted and even produced a tiny Comintern smile. For some reason I blushed—I hope my tan hid my confusion.

"But no, Davud," his mother said in a voice of delighted protest. "Pity, Davud, pity, please—you know you hate anything to do with . . ." She searched for the word and finally said, ". . . with *commerce*."

"What a big word, Betty, for such a delightful outing." To us he added, "Our house may not be much but I love it. It's where my grandfather lived and died and his father, Ottomans of the old school."

His mother, whom he kept calling Betty to her vexed amusement, puffed out her cheeks in mock impatience. "Ottoman? Yes, if that means your grandfather never worked a day in his life, denounced Ataturk constantly, much to our detriment, and lamented the good old days of eunuchs and smelly old wandering dervishes." She held her very large nose with a tanned finger and thumb to indicate distaste for the glamorous past.

Helena and I exchanged a quick glance to acknowledge this snobbish mother-son game of pretending to lament what one secretly plumes oneself over. We'd spotted this maneuver in other people and had already laughed about it.

As we were leaving, Betty shook her head operatically and said to Helena, "I can't imagine what sort of spell you've cast over my lazy, impractical, WHIMSICAL son!" (She shouted the "whimsical" while bugging her eyes at her son, or rather at her vaudeville partner).

When we were back at the Pera Palas and relaxing in its vast Edwardian lobby, an Orientalist version of a West End men's club, the Garrick on the Golden Horn, Helena said nothing beyond asking with a faint smile, "That dishy wog today, do you think he likes boys or girls?"

TRUE to his word Davud greeted our ferry on the long, windowed landing at Büyükada, which was decorated with Turkish words written in the outmoded Arabic script.

Davud gave us a big friendly wave and a dosed smile. He had Helena on one side and me on the other as he hurried us along, touching us both lightly on the shoulder. "We must hire a carriage to get out to the *yali*." Behind some stores, faced in unpainted wood like serfs' houses in a Tolstoyan village, lay a big taxi rank of horse-drawn phaetons, if that's what you call these open carriages with facing seats accommodating four and a convertible roof that can be raised. Most of them had shiny plastic-covered seats in an improbably bright green or eggplant with gold stars in their translucent depths, but some had proper sun-faded leather uphol-stery and suspended hands of Fatima or glass eyes on strings for good luck.

There were dozens of carriages inching their way up to the raised landing dock where we waited our turn and then boarded without needing to step up or down, though the carriage bounced on its springs under our sudden weight. Davud was careful to put Helena and me together on the seat that faced forward and then he sat opposite me, our knees nearly touching.

"I thought your great Ataturk had banned veils and burkas," Helena murmured, indicating with a twitch of her chin the women in the party just ahead of ours, all three sheathed in something black and synthetic that even covered their faces like some horrible cocoon.

"They're Arabs," Davud said. "Saudis, probably. They often come here during Ramadan, which we're less, uh, rigorous about observing. We're much more *laissez-aller* here."

As if on cue we could hear a muezzin, his bleating voice electrically amplified, calling the faithful to prayer, though none of the merchants in the stores we were trotting past seemed phased by the summons. When I mentioned that, Davud shrugged, as if my observation was uncool and touristy, though after a while he said, "Many of the people on the island are Jews. The Sultan took 20,000 Spanish Jews and many of them have summer houses here."

"When was that?" Helena asked. "After the war?"

Davud smiled. "In 1492. During the Inquisition."

"Help!" Helena cried, "He's going all historical on us. We can't bear pedants."

For once I wished Helena hadn't spoken for me.

"Wasn't a synagogue blown up recently in Istanbul?"

Helena asked next with a hint of aggressiveness in her voice, as if to darken Davud's rosy picture of Turkish tolerance.

Davud merely squinted and said, "Up here is the butcher we use, though I hope you're not squeamish about flies, which cover the meat, which hangs from hooks. No refrigeration. And there, that's where I buy the sour cherry juice we Turks affection. Do you say 'affection' or is that a verb only in French?"

"'Like' is what we say," I said, looking at him steadily.

"My English," he complained, shrugging.

"But it's excellent!" Helena protested as the official keeper of standard pronunciation. "Did you study in England?"

"I went to a little law school near London, just south of London, for a little semester. Not a known school, just a little—"

"In English men don't say *little*. We don't speak in diminutives," Helena announced.

Davud pretended he hadn't heard. "But I'm not studious. I don't like the law. I was homesick."

There was a cool sea breeze siphoning up through the trees as we climbed the leafy, hilly road that wound past the old yalis in their splendid gardens of roses and big, grandmotherly mauve hydrangeas. Some of the houses were set back behind fences of impressive iron staves tipped in gold, though others were smaller and leaned out over the pavement and looked modest and approachable like ski chalets. "Those shutters," Helena said, "have carved-out tulips."

"The flower we invented," Davud said. "When we

tried to conquer Vienna we failed, *twice*, but at least we did leave behind tulips—and coffee, which the human central system of nervous seems to crave." He appeared to be very pleased with the word *crave*, which he worked into the conversation again.

He was being gallant with Helena (though she was muttering again about pedantry) and deferential with me, but he also laced his beautiful manners with a certain coolness that was unmistakably aristocratic (if Helena heard me saying that, she would whoop with laughter, since she thinks Americans are clueless about the aristocracy).

I was intensely aware of his white hands on his knees—not exactly white, more the color of weak tea. The back of his hands and the top knuckles were covered with fine black hair, which seemed to me (how to say it?) somehow "fatherly" and "decent," as if they were a family doctor's hands and all they lacked were a stethoscope and a gold wedding band. His manner was tricky and dandified but his hands were honest and reassuring. The most natural thing in the world would have been to lean forward to kiss them.

The whole house had been kept closed for a long time, I imagined, and everything smelled of airless hot wood, of brass wiring and good tar soap. He and a reluctant old servant, whose nap we'd visibly interrupted, led us through. There must have been twenty rooms, each another half step down the hill toward the water's edge and a freshly painted boathouse.

The minute I saw the narrow entrance hall with its boot rack and coat tree I thought to myself, "I'm going to become so familiar with all this that breezing past it will become second nature. I'll soon be on cozy familial terms with these blue and white floor tiles, the ormolu grandfather clock so shallow it seems to be pressing itself against the wall like a hiding child, the silk shade dripping fringe over a green faience vase. My muscles will memorize where the step comes and how deep it is, where to find the switch without looking to turn on that outsize crystal chandelier hung with the million dusty Bohemian crystal lusters. I'll learn how to squeeze past this flotilla of armless slipper chairs covered in dusty rose silk to arrive at the sunroom that gives onto a secret garden.

The next sitting room was obviously "the Turkish corner" with its inscriptions in gilt Arabic calligraphy spelling out the ninety-nine names of Allah along the low cornice—or so Davud said, though he shrunk away comically from Helena's upraised warning finger. We looked at its brass hookah, its couch pressed up against one wall and its thick Persian carpet laid out for contemplation with woven patterns of fountains and paradisal flower baskets and its mirhab on the side, presumably, facing Mecca.

"Here's Madame's room," Davud said at the next door. We crossed it and he pulled back the royal blue satin curtains to illuminate a Venetian bed worthy to be an empress's sleigh, freighted with dozens of embroidered cushions the light blue of shadows on snow. The wall sconces were electrified candles backed by scalloped, antiqued mirrors narrow at the base and rounded and flared at the top. There were four, five, six! sconces and an enchanting three-mirror vanity table, all stoppered unguents and perfume atomizers in cut rose quartz. "You may think it's in dubious taste," Davud said, "but at least it's Late Ottoman kitsch. They liked everything French and English but they—or rather we—gave it that extra twist, to turn it into a sickly sweet bonbonnière, something to make you think of the harem and drugged sherbets of watermelon ice. And cruel. The cruelty is an important ingredient."

"Oh, you're such a ham!" Helena scolded. "Say what you will, it's heavenly. So feminine."

"Is there anything more feminine than a harem? Think of Ingres," and he leered comically and stroked an invisible handlebar mustache.

Here I've taken a little break from writing this up to greet my Bulgarian friend. There now, I feel much better. On with my Turkish delights. . . .

"Did your grandfather," Helena blurted out before she trailed off, wondering where her question might lead us, "keep a harem?"

"My great-great-grandfather did." He counted the generations off on his fingers starting with his thumb. "Yes, great, great, grand . . . he had many women. By the time my grandfather came along we Turkish men had entered an era of diminished expectations."

Helena and I could see by the twinkle in his eye that we were meant to laugh and we did.

"Now, Helena, if I may . . ."

"But you must!"

"You stay here for a moment in your pale-blue kitsch harem and I'll show Monsieur his austere little cubbyhole."

"All right," she drawled dubiously, though within an instant she'd danced around her room, flopped and was luxuriating on the heavily quilted bedspread; she looked like a very pretty cloud riding low over neatly tilled springtime fields.

Davud didn't say anything as he led me down one corridor and then another (I'm feeling dizzy for some reason). He waved the servant off. We crossed a garden, he opened a heavy wood door and once inside closed it and gave me a passionate kiss—yes, it felt as if someone had just pressed a fresh ripe mango over my face, that's how it felt, yes. Though I was twelve or fifteen years older than he was, suddenly he was whispering in my ear, "My little boy."

"Am I really?" I asked idiotically, an octave too high.

"Yes," he said, "that's what you are."

I said, "We'll take it—the house."

HE escorted us everywhere on the island in a carriage he retained for days on end. He showed us where the carriage drivers lived in makeshift cottages down in a valley surrounded by trees. He led us down a steep pathless hill to a tiny hidden beach where we swam and sunbathed in solitude. Later he invited us to lunch in a grove where a sort of witch with wild hair and dirty hands served us grilled lamb. Again we were quite alone.

He flirted with Helena so much and so convincingly that, despite her famous "gaydar," she said, "He's one for my side. He's one you'll never get."

But she also wondered if she'd ever "get" him. "Do you think I'm too fat for him?"

"You're not fat, " I insisted. "Anyway, you see how these Turkish men worship you—you're like their sultana Roxelana, the Russian. They never take their eyes off you."

She brightened up. "Did I tell you how the masseuse at that hammam near the Blue Mosque told me that her husband would give ten years of his life for one night with me?"

"No," I lied, so she'd have the pleasure of repeating it.

"I asked would he prefer me over that lovely French girl over there? I pointed out a *mannequin* the next slab over. But no, the masseuse said, she's as skinny as a boy! Madame is a *real* woman."

"Hear, hear!" I said.

What I daren't tell her was that Davud had put me in my austere cubbyhole because it had an outside door. He visited me every night after we three had spent a long wonderful day together, and he'd taken his leave, bowing at the waist in ironic salaams.

I'd yawn and stretch and murmur my bored assent while Helena parsed Davud, praised him for his looks and charm and speculated about his exaggerated interest in us. "He can't be that bored. Maybe he's a fortune hunter and he thinks I'm the other Helena," she said. "After all his mother pretended they were renting the yali out just this once because they were all heading off for Davos or Arosa or wherever, but yet here they still are."

"I'm sure you're right," I said.

"Right? Which part of what I just said, pray, is right in your opinion? You're hopeless about Davud. I think they need the money, that they're nouveau pauvre and fighting to keep up appearances. I love the yali but it's a wreck. Face it. My theory jibes with her asking us not to say we were renting but rather to pretend we're her guests. She's says it's not the Turkish custom to rent out homes. Then she said she doesn't want to declare our rent on her taxes. But she just doesn't want the other ladies at the country club to know she's hard-up."

"Oh," I moaned, "that *country club*." We'd seen a group of chubby, heavily painted Turkish subteens giggling and rushing into the country club, all wearing long-sleeved sweaters laden down with heavy gold appliqué. Davud had snorted something about *la jeunesse dorée*.

"No wonder he likes me given the competition," Helena said. "I'm blonde and sophisticated and I speak several languages, not one of those Bedouins in lamé jumpers."

I couldn't figure out how to end the evening except by kissing her on the forehead and miming sleep by resting my cheek on joined hands. "You're hopeless!" she shouted, then patted me vaguely and whispered, "Nighty-night." She withdrew into her pale blue chamber which at night, all six wall sconces alight, glowed like the inside of a pine branch on fire.

As soon as I was in my room someone locked the door, yes, locked it from the inside, someone naked and warm who pulled me to the bed. "I thought you'd never come," he said.

He held me and told me all the things he'd never confessed to anyone. I felt that no one had ever really listened to him—to his stories of school sports (he'd been a soccer champ), to his mixed feelings about his family's exalted military past, to his pride and regret that he was so caught up in the famous melancholy of Istanbul. He talked and talked while holding and probing all the most sensitive parts of my body while I listened, sometimes for hours.

I like men who are elegant in the drawing room and savage in the bedroom—imperious and demanding. Davud suited me perfectly. His torso—his whole body—was as hairy as the backs of his hands but with black glossy filaments that lay flat on his skin. By night he did things to me that were sometimes sharp and painful but that by day I nursed a bit sulkily when my shirt brushed against, say, a wounded nipple. I wore long-sleeved, high-collared shirts to hide the hickey or bruise. "Soon *you* will be wearing a burka!" Helena shouted. "Look at you, covered from chin to wrist."

"You know how sensitive to the sun—"

"—that new medication makes you," she said by weary rote.

She didn't like the idea of pills of any sort, even pre-scribed ones.

NOR does she like my opium pipe. In fact she violently disapproves of it. Today she let herself into my apartment without knocking (I must get around to telling her to phone first). She sniffed the air and said, "What are you doing lying in that *clothes hamper*?" When she dislikes something she pronounces it with all the disdain of a Lady Bracknell.

It's true I've filled a big osier-woven hamper with quilts and pillows. "It's my nest, Helena. You have your bed and your cats. It comforts me on rainy days . . . "

"And that smell of cheap perfume you buy down at the chemist's. When you spray it about—you can't possibly *like it*—I know you mumble mumble . . ."

"What?"

"The opium smell, you're trying to disguise it."

"Picasso called it the least stupid smell in the world."

"Mumble."

"What?"

"Whatever that *fucking* means! The *effect*"—here she was over-articulating—"certainly doesn't render its victims intelligent. You're the only person I've ever heard of in Greece who could even find opium. Hash, yes, but opium never. I could murder that Boris for getting you addicted to it."

Helena snooped around the room with a proprietorial air. She does own our house and I do merely rent, but she hasn't grasped the concept of a renter's privacy. She's always leaning over the balcony above my laundry patio where I like to take the sun and read the *Herald Tribune*. Or she traces a finger through the plaster dust on my desk; it falls so fast I can't keep up with it.

"I was just daydreaming about that nice Davud we met in—"

"*Nice!* Davud? Devious wretch, you mean. And I'd hardly dignify your stupor by calling it 'daydreaming.' Americans certainly have a gift for euphemism." And without another word she rushed off, accompanied by three of her skittering cats like Hecuba on a rampage. I felt tempted to pull the hamper lid down over me.

BY "devious wretch" Helena perhaps is referring to a Sunday (the Turks observe our weekly calendar) when Davud showed up for our daily carriage ride with a young woman, thin and fastidiously dressed in dark colors and a Missoni sweater as muted and subtle as the old Kilim in my bedroom—no lamé appliqués for her. Her name was Belkis. Davud said in a soft voice, "Belkis is my fiancée and I thought it might be amusing—"

"Your *what*?" Helena exclaimed.

"We will be married next spring," Davud said, closing his eyes as he spoke.

Belkis was lovely; she asked me questions with a sweetness and curiosity that seemed a perfect emblem of today's evolved Turkish woman. I took their engagement in good stride since we gay men never expect things to work out anyway. My good grace was remarkable given that I had the most to lose or at least was the most affected, but Helena had been given no way to know that. She spoke little and then in icy tones. She barely looked at Belkis and never smiled at her.

Davud had what he called the "genial" idea (again a Gallicism meaning "brilliant") to hire us all donkeys to clamber up the highest hill to an old Byzantine monastery. "This is where the deposed Byzantine princes were imprisoned."

"I'm glad to know the cruelty started way back then,"

Helena said, tipping her head back and staring loftily at Davud as though he were personally responsible for centuries of unpleasantness.

"I warned you," Davud called out gaily. "Sweetness *and* cruelty!" He cracked a huge smile.

Madame was not amused. She said she'd skip the monastery and donkey. For once Helena wasn't a good sport.

That evening as soon as we were alone after a long, tense dinner by the sea, Helena exploded: "I'm sick of bits of charred octopus and electrocuted guppies and cucumbers in vinegar longing to be pickles."

"But Davud says the Turkish 'kitchen' rivals the French and the Chinese."

"I don't care what that bore says." We had a very long debriefing that night about the "faithless Turk," as he was now called. "How *dare* he not tell us he was engaged? He obviously likes them thin the way they all do. Well, good riddance. It's obviously an arranged marriage—she's even more of a bore than he is."

"I thought she was sweet," I hazarded, "though she didn't say much."

"Oh you did, did you? Sweet? Another American euphemism for a colorless little pushover." She listened to herself and then added grumpily, "I could have pushed her over that cliff when she was trying out poetic modern dance steps to celebrate the sunset. And by the way, have you noticed how his treats are always penny ice creams whereas ours are whole electrocuted squid dinners?"

Soon we were both roaring with laughter over the

very idea of the squid dinner. I didn't mind lingering with Helena for once. She needed the comfort after the blow she'd received, and I assumed that when I returned to my bedroom it would be empty.

But no, he was there, his face, neck and hands tanned a dark Darjeeling brown from the day while his body remained jasmine pale. The wait and possibly the tensions of the day made him rougher and more eager than ever before, as if this time he wanted to climb right inside me like an incubus—or djinn.

Afterwards (or rather between bouts, for he was tireless) he told me that his engagement meant nothing, it was just a formality, that Belkis was a cousin and a delight but that his marriage would in no way diminish his feelings for me. This part of the story is all a bit vague, like a dream . . .

"In fact," he said, pulling my whole body against his so that our nipples matched and our genitals touched and my feet were stepping on his (he was taller) and his words, which smelled of my semen, were breathing right into my face, "in fact I want you to move here and live here. There's the University of the Bosphorus out by the Rumeli Tower, and I've spoken to the dean and they'd be thrilled to have someone of your caliber—though at first it would be just a part-time position . . ."

NOW, let me put just a bit more of this in my pipe. I feel like the nineteenth-century French traveler and novelist Pierre Loti who wrote *The Disenchanted*, a wonderful dreamy book about the oppression of women in Turkey. In the novel he's always meeting up with these three veiled ladies in a safe house and there they all drink tea and discuss their souls. Loti loved drag of any sort—pharonic, military, courtly—and would get himself up in a fez and baggy trousers and a scimitar and smoke opium and drink sugared tea in that melancholy little café above the Golden Horn next to the old Ottoman cemetery. We went out there once to the Eyüb Mosque and saw twelve-year-olds running around in Zorro capes and drum majors' hats, getting ready for their circumcisions. It was Davud who took us there and pointed out that the six or seven unmarked tombstones nearest the café were those of executioners who feared that if they were identified their graves might be desecrated by the families of their victims. Davud taught us all the symbols on the Ottoman tombs—the various stone fezzes on top of steles that indicated notables of differing degree, the stone veils that commemorated virgins. When we were alone he liked to call me his "Little Loti." Come to think of it, I once visited Loti's house back in France, now a museum, in Rochefort on the Atlantic coast. Loti had had an entire miniature mosque built inside so that he could lounge around in his vaporous trousers and turbans and smoke opium while outside the winter storms raged.

There! Now I do feel like a little Loti if that's the plural of lotus, floating in my hamper as in a stagnant pond.

I was unable to accept Davud's offer. I didn't want to give up my good pension nor the solitary pleasures of my snug little Chicago apartment. Much as I adored Davud and shivered when he touched me, I'd lived too long as a hermit and celibate to endure his embraces (all night every night). I longed for a whole night alone— "craved" it, as he would say. I wanted a virginal veil to be dropped over my stele. My body—every surface, every orifice—felt chafed, invaded, and his insistent voice had replaced my own thoughts. For a while all I could hear when I thought was his voice talking about Belkis and how she'd been raised by his family, of his grandfather's death in the *yali* and his way of refusing to relax into death—how he'd sat up rigidly in bed until death had felled him suddenly as if with a scimitar blade. He talked of his loneliness in law school in England, how his "exile" there had made him realize, not altogether happily, how much he depended on his family legend, how sometimes he thought he wasn't really an individual, not in the way an Englishman might be— that he was tribal before he was individual. That voice, alternating with his fingers probing me and his bites wounding me so sweetly, consumed me completely— ate up every last fiber of *my* individuality.

Nor could I envision living in Istanbul, learning an impossible new language all dactyls and slurred s's and sustained umlauts. I'd be a back-street mistress to a married Turk, who was always restless and on the prowl because his pride as a fallen grandee was permanently wounded and his well-tailored pockets were permanently empty. He had no profession but idler and he couldn't afford that.

And then for me there was Helena. Her father had

just died and she was bereft. Her bitch of a mother had actually told her at the graveside, "You know why Daddy was so disappointed in you? Because you've become so grotesquely fat."

I knew she'd feel terribly betrayed if she ever discovered my intense secret two-month affair with Davud, especially since in the beginning she'd thought he was pursuing her. Which would be worse—admitting that her gaydar was on the blink? Or confronting my faithlessness?

She'd already remarked on the dark circles under my eyes and once she'd seen a love bite on my neck and said, "Been sneaking off to the carriage drivers' encampment, I suppose." She raised an eyebrow.

I'd let my secret go on too long. She'd never trust me again if I confessed to it at this late date. Besides, even back then, twenty years ago—more!—we were already talking about living together somewhere, some time. "When we retire!" we cried, never imagining that day would come so soon.

She's such fun. We always laugh a lot, though lately she's tired and depressed in this eternal rain. But soon it will be spring and we'll go tootling off in her car out into the countryside where wildflowers will be rioting like Bacchantes on every slope. We'll buy our whole lamb for Easter and carry it up all our steps on our shoulder like Isaac and it will be such a lark.

Last night she walked in on me as I was dozing, foundered in my cozy hamper, and she dragged me out of it, rooted around in the blankets until she found my black lump of opium. She broke it into bits and flushed it down the toilet, though she's the one who forbids anyone to flush toilet paper lest it stop up the narrow pipes (I find soiled paper in a waste basket sort of disgusting). Then, still in a fury she saw my old copy of *The Isle of Princes* and shredded it with her hands and cast it into the fire. I was high and indifferent though I didn't much appreciate her bossiness to the degree I could take it in at all. Opium dissolves frontiers and makes every country delightful and calm.

"You've got to come back to the present," she said, and she picked up my ruby-red glass and hurled it to the floor. "That lazy Turkish runt wasn't such a jewel. He didn't even like men. You remember that fake list of damages they put together at the end of the summer just to soak us some more? Even that corrupt sinister Cansen stood behind them. What's wrong with you? If you're going to dwell on the past it should at least be a *viable memory.*"

Her words hung in the air and soon we were weeping with laughter over the absurdity of the whole concept of viable nostalgia, choking with great gulps of laughter, though she might have judged the situation differently if I'd disclosed my full deceit.

Yet truth be told I'm no longer certain about this whole story. How much of it did I read in Ozbekhan's book or Loti's and how much of it have I been filling in during one of my long winter pipe dreams?